POETIC
JUSTICE

BOOKS IN THIS SERIES

POETIC JUSTICE

INTRUSION

FRAN RAYA

The Book Guild Ltd

First published in Great Britain in 2022 by
The Book Guild Ltd
Unit E2 Airfield Business Park,
Harrison Road, Market Harborough,
Leicestershire. LE16 7UL
Tel: 0116 2792299
www.bookguild.co.uk
Email: info@bookguild.co.uk
Twitter: @bookguild

Typeset in Aldine401 BT

Printed and bound in Great Britain by CPI Group (UK) Ltd, Croydon, CR0 4YY

ISBN 978 1915352 149

British Library Cataloguing in Publication Data.
A catalogue record for this book is available from the British Library.

I wish to dedicate this fifth book in my ongoing series to its protagonist; the demonic, dynamic and decadent Randal Forbes.

Without my theatrical imagination he would not have been actualized. I truly don't know how I created him. He is unrelenting.

The power of invention is so rewarding. Authors thrive on visualization and Randal Forbes encapsulates innovation.

Randal Forbes calls his dark powers 'the gift' and his radiating eyes are the windows of his phenomenal psychic domination.

Randal's daughter Roxanne has proved she is also worthy of her inheritance, and has used her own 'gift' to severely injure their main rival, Carlton Flint.

In this fifth book of the series, there is relentless intrusion. Telepathic crime with a paranormal edge is Randal's defence. He has a twisted sense of poetic justice, so he will remove any obstacles he feels are in his fiendish path.

Randal Forbes has a dark side so powerful that only a rival with the same 'gift' will be able to challenge him.

Will Carlton Flint recover and do just that?

1

Carlton Flint was dreaming. He was in a landscaped garden with the most exquisite blooms. His wife, Francine, was sitting on the lush, green lawn, with a red gingham tablecloth beneath her.

She opened the wicker picnic basket and brought out an assortment of mouth-watering food. A crusty French bread with homemade cherry jam. Flaky seeded crackers with crumbly cheese, laced with cranberries. A freshly baked sponge cake layered with strawberries and cream. A bottle of chilled, pink champagne. Carlton heard the cork pop and then she filled two flutes with the brisk, sparkling wine.

"Cheers," she said with a perfect smile. "Here's to us."

They clinked glasses and laughed. The sun was a circular ball of heat glowing conceitedly in its deep, blue sky. Carlton covered his eyes with his hand to shield them from the intense rays.

Then suddenly a dark cloud appeared on the horizon, moving towards them at a daunting, rapid pace. It searched for the sun and totally eclipsed its radiance, sucking the heat out of the atmosphere and sending a chilly indifferent pocket of dense air that seemed to linger over their immediate locality.

1

Carlton shivered and rubbed his arms. He reached for Francine to keep her warm, but she began to fade, her features melting into a faceless blob. A hideous, blurred mask. Then her body disappeared, leaving just a faint outline of her shapely posture.

"Francine? Francine! Where are you? Where've you gone!" he cried inside, but he could not form the words with his mouth, only in his mind.

He struggled to stand up, but he was super-glued to the lawn. A mass of visible water vapour hovered right above him and descended like some malignant meteorite before it crash-landed on the back of his head. Then everything went black.

★★★

Dr Winston Ramsey thought he detected rapid eye movements behind Carlton's closed lids. He lifted up the left eyelid and shone a light inside. Nothing. He did the same with the right one and turned to Francine, shaking his head.

"Sorry, Mrs Flint, but I was looking for signs of response. Sadly, I was mistaken, but we will do everything we can. Miracles sometimes happen, even on life support. We have to remain positive. I've seen a case before where the patient was comatose, and quite frankly had very little chance of survival, but he woke up with all his senses intact. So, let's see what transpires. I assure you that we're all doing our very best for your husband.

"I know you are, Dr Ramsey, and my family are eternally grateful."

He did not want to mention Clive Hargreaves, or his enigmatic employer. That would not go down well as an example of the aforementioned miraculous recovery. Because the name that had been repeatedly echoing in Winston's head, since he witnessed the possible assistance in Clive's supernatural revival, was the very same person that Carlton Flint's family were taking to the judicial cleaners.

Randal Forbes!

Winston had looked closely into Randal's background since that mind-blowing day. The more he discovered, the more he believed in the unbelievable. His colleagues did not. But they had not seen the alien glint of optical interference. They had not felt the bubbling action of heat, running in hot-blooded beads over Randal's slippery skin. His blood pressure so ridiculously off the scale, so extreme that he should have been spark out, let alone sprawled prostrate on a chair, struggling to breathe.

Randal was in a worse state than the phenomenally revived Clive Hargreaves, who had been knocking on heaven's door and about to be admitted. He was at the head of the solemn queue of extinction but then suddenly spiritually relegated back to his earthly plain, with his mortal coil well intact. Winston frowned as he came to a very non-viable conclusion.

I'm now positive that Randal had a helping, unorthodox hand in Clive's restoration. There's absolutely no other way of viewing that regeneration. No other way at all. Hargreaves was dying and brought back to life! Impossible! In this case? Probable!

★★★

Randal's son Ryan had also been suspicious of his father's, and adopted sister's, mysterious powers, with regard to Carlton's comatose state. When he had read the article in the *Daily Announcer* his heart began to hammer against his chest wall. Roxanne had told the reporter, quote, "I don't want to talk about the starman's head." That glaring statement jumped out at Ryan and had grabbed him by the throat, until he'd reached a stage of nervous strangulation.

I knew it! I knew there was something in it! Dad and Roxanne meant it! Mum was wrong! It wasn't a game! It was a plan! They spoke about killing the starman! And now I know what they meant!

He had first heard the reference to the starman when he had unintentionally eavesdropped on that weird conversation between his father and Roxanne. They'd spoke about wanting him dead but to keep it all away from Clive, so that they would not upset him again. His mother, Alison, thought he was being dramatic when he told her, but Ryan had always felt there was some kind of powerful communication system that Randal and Roxanne bought into. Something they call 'the gift'.

Did they cause Carlton's horrific accident? But how could they? Surely his father would not bring this intrusive, constant, bad press to their own doorstep? Why would he put his company, Astral TV, in the tangled mess of litigation? It would be insane to sabotage the machinery that caused a huge, suspended screen to detach itself from the ceiling and crash down on Carlton's head.

Ryan needed to talk to his father privately because he could not carry on with these unsavoury thoughts in his head. He had to know if there was some kind of unspoken collusion between Randal and Roxanne that had contributed towards Carlton's present life-threatening condition.

Ryan heard Randal's keys rattle in the front door lock. He was home early and everyone was otherwise occupied, so now was the perfect time to approach him, if there was ever going to be an ideal moment. Randal stormed into the hallway with a face like thunder as he meditated grimly.

Damn these inquisitions! The paparazzi police! Go to hell and burn, you morons!

"Alison? Alison! Are you home?" he barked, but there was no reply as he walked from room to room.

"Mum's in the back with Amber and Roxanne, sorting out some plants. We've been shopping to a garden centre," clarified Ryan, as he appeared in the kitchen doorway, his little handsome face reflecting his acute anxiety.

"Have you seen those bloody cameras outside? It's endless! *Endless!* I hope they didn't bother your mum or upset you all. If they did, I'll sue the tossers!" he raved, forgetting his language in front of his young son and turning the air cobalt-blue.

"We got out of the car and covered our faces with our hands," Ryan explained, his resolve weakening by the second.

"Did they follow you? Did they? Because, if they did, I won't be responsible for my wrath!" snapped Randal, with sparking eyes that looked as if they would ignite into laser beams of light.

"A few of them did," whispered Ryan.

"Did they now? I'll give them something to write about!"

Ryan's objectives were fading fast. His father's foul mood deterred him from his purpose. Should he take the proverbial bull by the horns and risk a question-and-answer conversation in order to satisfy his confusion? How could four words be so confounding? 'The starman' and 'the gift'.

Randal stomped into the kitchen and filled the kettle. He slammed it down onto its base and nearly fused the switch in the process, as he flicked it on with unnecessary force.

"I wouldn't mind," he continued to rave. "The news on the world's political stage is so dire! Famine, unrest, war-mongering! But who's grabbing the headlines? Me, Dean, Astral TV and away-with-the-fairies Flint!" What does that really say about our celebrity-obsessed media? Witless, uninformed, drivelling, fatuous cretins! All of them! Every single one!"

Ryan abandoned his much-needed discussion. His father was furious and had that intimidating visual assertion in his molten eyes: those flickering yellow sparks, like hot coals after the fire had been stoked.

Randal suddenly felt a strong, negative vibration which he realised was Ryan's fearful curiosity. He inhaled his son's frightened and discontented scent and looked directly at his startled features. It took Randal a few seconds to analyse Ryan's suspicious conclusions.

This is all I need! My son suspects foul play and I've got to make it right, he groaned to himself.

"I have to talk to you, Ryan. I need to explain why I'm so mad. I'm sorry if I've upset you. I didn't mean to."

Ryan's confusion stepped up another notch.

"Come here and sit with me at the table," requested Randal.

Ryan sat awkwardly next to his father, his whole body rigid and on edge. He truly did not know what to expect. He needed to comprehend the reality of the bewildering situation. Randal took a deep breath before he spun his most lengthy, fabricated, inventive yarn to date.

"Now listen carefully, Ryan. I know you're very confused, but here's the thing. Even though Carlton Flint was successful and pulled in massive viewing figures for Astral TV, we never really liked each other. I went along with the programme because Dean was so enthusiastic about the full project, and I didn't want to let him down by rejecting his discovery. Then, Roxanne met Carlton at my office, and he upset her," he fibbed.

"He upset Roxanne? How, Dad?"

"He kept going on about Maxine and Saul and how she would learn to forget them. I don't think he meant it in a bad way, but she became very disturbed after his advice. I had a few words with him about it and things got really out of hand. I nearly hit him. Clive was upset with me for losing my temper in front of Roxanne, and rightly so. After that I nicknamed him the starman; a bit obvious, but it suited him, and it was a way of making him less important," concocted Randal.

"What happened after that?" enquired Ryan, naively.

"Roxanne asked me how the starman read people's minds. Well, that's what she thought he did, even though it was pure astrology. I told her he had 'the gift'. Then she asked me if she would ever have 'the gift' and to make her feel better, I said it was possible. So, then she wanted to use 'the gift' to get rid of Carlton. She hated him that much. I went along with the sham.

I know it was a weird thing to do but it helped her heal and come out of her low mood whenever we played the silly game. Even Maxine's family couldn't help her, so when a child is so disturbed you have to do whatever you can to make them feel safe and loved. Sometimes the craziest of things can bring them out of their sadness," he schemed.

Ryan felt all his muscles unwind and the tension leave his taut body. The relief was enormous, but there was still the feeling that Roxanne could read his mind.

"I understand, Dad, but she seems to be able to answer my thoughts. I'm thinking something and she jumps in as if I've asked her out loud. It happens all the time; a lot," he frowned.

"With me too," admitted Randal. "She's very tuned in. Perhaps she has got 'the gift' in some ways. Slightly psychic, like me, and your mum can be at times. We've a certain chemistry together, an understanding of all things spiritual. It's in your mum's music, and a lot of my books and song lyrics. Roxanne has that same awareness. Remember, her parents were gifted in the arts and were heavily into that kind of thing. Especially Maxine. I had many a conversation with her about it," he lied, and lied again.

"Oh, I get it now. I was really worried about all of this. I didn't know what was going on. I heard you talk about the starman once, and it sounded scary. But now I understand," he acknowledged.

"That's OK, Ryan. If I were you, I'd feel exactly the same. It's been a bad time all round with lots of misunderstandings. I'm glad we've managed to clear up your doubts and worries about what you thought you heard. Now you know it was all make-believe. Don't ever be afraid to ask me about something you don't get."

"I know you're mad over it all, Dad. Everyone's after you for money so I didn't really want to bring this up, but now you've told me everything. I'm really sorry that you're upset. I know it's not your fault that Carlton's ill. I wish they'd all leave our family alone. I'm getting a lot of stick at school over it. It's been hard," confessed Ryan.

Randal was so relieved that Ryan believed him but felt enormously guilty that his ten-year-old son had been innocently dragged into the whole sorry mess of unwanted publicity.

"I promise you, Ryan, that this will be over soon and we'll just get on with our lives," he stressed.

"What about Carlton?"

"What about him?"

"What if... what if he never wakes up? Ever."

"We'll face that, if, and when, it happens."

"But if he dies then it's not an accident anymore. They'll say it's murder and you're to blame. Dean, too. So, what then?" gulped Ryan.

"If he dies, it won't be murder. It'll be accidental death and I'll be able to prove it. Believe me. Anyway, try not to think about it all. You never know, he might wake up one day. Clive did. Remember?"

"That was amazing, Dad! Uncle Clive was dying."

"Well, there you are then. Now, do you fancy a large chocolate milkshake, made the Randal Forbes magic way?"

"Yeah... that'd be ace." Ryan smiled, his thoughts becoming normal again.

"Right then, just relax and think of something nice," advised Randal. "The more you think positive, the quicker it'll happen."

"I'm thinking I want all the reporters to go away."

"Well, you keep thinking on those lines all the time. Thoughts create circumstances, you know."

"If it works, does that mean I'll have 'the gift' as well?" Ryan grinned.

"You're a Forbes, aren't you?" Randal smiled as he cogitated. *You're a Forbes. Without the inheritance and with no more questions!*

Spencer Forbes bit on his solid, silver pen and thought long and hard about his case for the prosecution. He knew he was dicing with great danger by representing Techscreen, who were countersuing Astral TV.

By rights, he should be acting for Randal, who was bringing legal action against Techscreen, for the alleged faulty service they had provided. The result was the destabilisation of the mount, and large screen, that had subsequently crashed down on Carlton's head, putting him in his present somnolent state with extensive brain damage.

Spencer's terror of Randal's tyrannous stewardship, and any malicious revenge, was surprisingly put on a bold back-burner. It had been overtaken by his absolute horror and rage at Carlton's life-threatening infirmity.

He really did not know if this so-called accident was malicious, deliberate or sinful on Randal's part, or whether it had been a straight-forward shoddy installation. All he knew was that Carlton had been there for him at his lowest point, and now he had to be unwavering in his legal support for Francine Flint and her two daughters.

The Forbes family were disgusted with Spencer. His father, Randal's Uncle Ashley, could not believe his son's betrayal, and visited Spencer to admonish him.

"What are you thinking of? Randal and Dean are going through hell and high water over this whole issue and need our unwavering support! I don't understand you, Spencer! In fact, I'm ashamed of you!" exclaimed Ashley.

"Dad, you don't get it. Please don't ask me to explain because you're not going to like the justification," claimed Spencer.

"Try me!" blazed Ashley. "I'm all ears!"

Spencer sighed very deeply. How to explain? Where to begin? It was now or never. It was about time they all knew.

"Randal's not what the family perceives him to be. He's devious and disingenuous. Please believe me on this one. I would not rest easy representing him. Carlton Flint is an upright, righteous man, who helped me out of my depression, a severe mental illness caused by Randal, and all the unsavoury, corrupt, woeful and evil circumstances that define him."

"*Evil?* You're telling me that Randal's *evil*? He's a wonderful son to my dear brother, Edward! A loyal, outstanding husband and father! A philanthropist! A benefactor! A genius in his own field! What are you saying? I can't believe my ears!" he wailed.

"I've got proof gathered over the years. I've followed his trail of destruction. Dad, please, I can't disclose the full extent of his crimes. You wouldn't believe me anyway. Just like you won't accept this tiny fraction of his transgression."

His father shook his head in disbelief.

Spencer carried on regardless. "All you need to know is that I'm representing the true, injured party. I have to do this, Dad. I simply have to do this!" he repeated passionately.

Ashley shook his head once more. "Why has it taken you so long to disclose this so-called evidence to me? Why have you never discussed the whole matter before? Why now? If it's been eating away at you, why have you let it fester without consulting me or your mother? It doesn't make any sense, Spencer!"

"I've chosen now because I can't live in the shadows anymore in fear of his reprisal. I have to make a stand even if it could trigger a dangerous response. I've spent too much time quaking with apprehension over his menacing antagonism. Well, no more! No more! No matter what!"

"I still can't make any sense of this! Your Uncle Edward and Aunty Margaret are terribly upset. I don't know what to tell them. I'm at a complete loss," moaned Ashley, scratching his head with agitation.

"Just tell them that I've been allocated the case, and I have to take what I'm given, or else my position in this company will be jeopardised. Tell them it's not my fault. I'm dancing to my superior's tune and nepotism is not allowed."

"You know this will split our family in two, don't you? Not just the Forbes side. Dean is Dottie's son, and her sister, Margaret, is Randal's mother, in case you've forgotten! There are cousins on either side involved here. Your disloyalty is breath-taking! I honestly believe that you're still unwell. Look how you behaved at Christmas, and after that! We were all worried sick about you. You disappeared off the face of the earth, and wouldn't talk to any of us," preached Ashley.

"I know, and that was all down to Randal. I was terrified that he would come after me," stipulated Spencer.

"Come after you for what? *For what?*" exclaimed Ashley.

"I'd found him out. He knew I'd been involved in a plan to discredit him. He realised that I'd worked alongside the relevant police authorities who wanted to charge him with the most abominable crimes but couldn't prove it beyond reasonable doubt."

"Oh, dear God! This is disastrous! Randal's just celebrated his birthday. He's thirty-three years old. It's taken you all this time to reveal why you've always felt uneasy in his company: this cock-and-bull story to justify years of rivalry and antagonism between you both! Do you think we've forgotten the sarcasm and disrespect you've always shown him, and vice-versa? Your brother James thinks it's plain old envy on your part. He told us that you were always jealous – way, way back, when you were all kids together. He feels you resent standing in Randal's shadow so your main defence is that of contempt. How do you expect Randal to be cordial and benevolent towards you if you're constantly and obsessively looking for the worst in him? He knows you're jealous of his achievements, and now, insult with injury, you wish to additionally discredit him to the world at large. I'm bloody speechless," groaned Ashley.

"Dad, nothing I say will get you to understand the hell I've been going through. There's a catalogue of victims, an endless list of suffering souls who've been murdered and maimed in the name of Randal Forbes. You've no idea! If I were to reveal it all to you, you'd pull your hair out! You'd never be able to look at him in the same way ever again! I mean, have you ever noticed his eyes?"

"What am I supposed to be looking for, Spencer? He has the same eyes as me, your Uncle Edward and even yourself. We all have the Forbes colouring. Red hair and grey eyes. What's the big deal with that?"

"Our eyes don't glow when we're annoyed!"

Ashley was beginning to fear for Spencer's sanity. His explanation had gone way beyond disloyal to delusional. Now he was making a mental roster of psychiatrists who could help his son.

Spencer knew only too well that his father would react in this disbelieving manner. That is why he had held the catastrophic cards close to his heart. He had always been unwilling to reveal the infernal essence that characterised Randal's treacherous trail of homicidal violation. It was his own fault. He should have disclosed it to both sides of Randal's family, right from its transgressive start. He should have brought them all into the pernicious picture so they could see for themselves the absolute extent of Randal's psychic psychosis.

Now it was too late, but not too delayed for him to make amends for Carlton, or any other victim with the misfortune to fall under Randal's dark jurisdiction. If anything should befall Spencer in the process, his father would realise the verity of his revelations, and Randal's disguised, demonic footprint in all of their lives.

"I don't know where we go from here," stated Ashley. "Do you expect me to believe that Randal has some kind of satanic disposition?"

"Well, if the cap fits."

"You seriously want me to agree with you over this nonsensical hocus-pocus?"

"Do you remember years ago, when Randal was a child? When Alice Hardman came personally to warn Uncle Edward and Aunty Margaret about his evil aura?"

"You mean the unbalanced headmistress who committed suicide by jumping, stark-naked, into the school swimming pool? She was deranged!" spluttered Ashley.

"You think so? He made her strip off her clothes, jump off the diving board and drown."

"He *made* her! How the hell did he *make* her do that, for heaven's sake?"

"With his mind, Dad. He gets inside people's heads and controls them."

"Oh, God! What else? I mean, is there anything more?" asked Ashley sardonically.

"There's his bisexuality for a start. Do you know that he's been in a physical relationship with Clive Hargreaves since they were teenagers?"

"Now I've heard it all! I'm seriously scared for your mental welfare. As if Alison would put up with that!" shouted Ashley.

"She doesn't know. He's hidden it well. Look, Dad, I'm not crazy, even though you think I am. Mark my words, one day you'll all realise that everything I'm telling you is the truth."

"The truth is, Spencer, that you need urgent help!" spluttered Ashley.

Spencer carried on regardless of his father's disbelief. "No, Dad, you're wrong! Until judgement day comes, I'll continue with my crusade. I'm prosecuting Randal's company, Astral TV and hopefully compensating the Flint family with a substantial award of money, so that Carlton can continue to have the private medical care he so rightfully deserves," concluded Spencer, as his father stormed out of the door with a face like thunder and a heavy heart.

★★★

13

Roxanne Dawn Forbes sat at her writing desk composing some more of her poems. She really wanted to create a short story and was thinking about all sorts of ideas for her first attempt. But mostly she wanted to impress Randal. In fact, she felt it was imperative to please him.

Since her disastrous attempt at removing Carlton had failed, she felt frustrated, displeased and angry with the outcome. She was also full of remorse and guilt about the legal position she had unintentionally put her father and Dean in, and all the subsequent damaging publicity it had evoked.

Why are you still alive, starman? I wanted to show my daddy I could use 'the gift' to kill you! I want him to be proud of me and now he's in big trouble. I didn't want all this bad stuff. I'm a good girl really.

Randal was at home and ready to appease his special offspring. She needed him and his constant reassurance. He stood in the doorway watching her write and cocked his head to one side to study her. How could he blame her? Such a precious prize! Roxanne spun round in the usual responsive fashion as she perceived his presence behind her.

"Daddy! I've just had a really, really good idea for a story!"

"Have you now?" he replied, and walked over to her.

"I have. It's about the starman. I can write him away and then I'll be happy even though it's not true."

Randal frowned. He did not want her dwelling on her first unsuccessful but well-meaning injurious performance of 'the gift'.

"You know, pumpkin; I think we should forget about him for now. He doesn't matter one little bit," he said softly.

"But I messed up, and now you and Dean are the bad ones, when it was me who caused it all," she replied, her bottom lip wobbling.

"You did what you needed to do and I'm proud of you because it was still an amazing result. Don't worry your pretty little head about any of it."

"Uncle Clive doesn't know it was me, does he?" she asked woefully.

"Not at all. Nobody knows. Just you and me. Now come here and give your daddy a big hug because he's had a rubbish day."

Roxanne instantly abandoned her story and ran into Randal's arms. "Daddy."

"Yes, pumpkin?"

"Can we make all the bad people outside go away? We can use 'the gift' properly to get rid of them. Oh, please? I'll feel lots better then. They're here every day and I hate them."

Randal looked at her compassionately. *I love her so much it hurts, my precious chosen daughter. Eight material years old but ethereally ancient.*

"No, pumpkin. We can't use 'the gift' so openly. It's too dangerous. We need to be more discreet."

"Discreet?"

"Careful. We don't want to make people too aware of our powers. We'll use them when we need to. Not when it doesn't really count."

"But all those horrid people standing outside our house and sitting on the wall, waiting to take our photos! And one big, ugly man forced me to talk into his microphone and I wouldn't, but he still kept on and on about it. All of them hate you and Dean. They're on the side of the starman. Uncle Clive's upset again because they're calling the office over and over to speak to him, because they can't speak to you. And it's all my fault!" she wailed, bursting into floods of tears.

Randal hugged her very tightly. He kissed the top of her head repeatedly.

"No, shush now. It's not your fault at all. If anyone's to blame then it's the starman. Boasting that he's got 'the gift' and his way's best. Stirring everything up," he confirmed with an unsettling, luminous glaze in his eyes. How dare they upset his priceless child?

"But—"

"But nothing. Now here's what we do," he clarified, gently stroking the strands of glossy, red hair away from her damp cheeks with his thumbs. "We'll get through all of this together and we'll win. But if things get really nasty, that's when we'll use 'the gift' to stop it all. Whoever's causing the problem. That's a promise. So, there's nothing for you to get upset about. Is there now?"

Roxanne sniffed and Randal reached inside his trouser pocket for his handkerchief. "Blow into this and wipe your pretty little nose."

She blew and blew dramatically, with another extra blow for effect, and looked up at him through identical eyes.

"Better now?"

"Much better now, Daddy."

"Good. Now, let's have a look at your poems. You know I love reading them," he encouraged.

"I've written another six, with a possible seven."

"Six with a possible seven, eh? Well, that sounds good to me."

As Randal admired her work he fumed inwardly. He would have no conscience whatsoever in using his powers on lesser mortals who persisted with this unwanted intrusion. And that included Spencer. So be it on his own head. Family or not!

★★★

Clive Hargreaves slammed down the telephone on another prying journalist. *This is getting ridiculous now!*

As Randal's agent, he had to use all his diplomatic, professional skills to ward them off without incurring worse publicity, but even that was not working. He had never in all his time as Randal's representative known such remorseless and relentless intrusion.

It was even more taxing than the questions thrown at them by the police authorities after some of Randal's homicidal performances, due to them both being, in some way or other, connected to the deceased. At least that was a singular examination. Their statements were taken and that was the end of it. Whatever suspicion they may have had about Randal's involvement was unproven.

How could he ever be charged? He was never there, and even the odd time he was in reasonable proximity to the crime; he was still not face to face. So, his paranormal offences remained unsolved and became historical, rather than accusatory.

Clive was still not completely sure if Carlton's infirmity was the work of Randal's powerful legacy or just a defective installation on behalf of the Techscreen engineer. Randal was a good actor even though he'd looked totally shocked on the night of that fateful broadcast. Facing a monumental lawsuit would not deter him from his wicked objective if he was darkly aroused. Clive meditated.

He could effectuate an atomic war if he thought it was needed!

Clive had to take into consideration Roxanne: that beautiful, exquisite child who had deeply touched his heart. Underneath the little-girl exterior was a powerhouse of psychic potential, soaking up the dark arts inside her father's home-grown, tainted philosophy. But she also had her own daredevil state of government without his tuition. Clive frowned. Then his heart skipped a beat. Then another one.

No! Surely not! But where was she on the night of Carlton's final programme? At home with Alison, Ryan and Amber! Watching the show! Randal boasts to me about Roxanne's ability to move objects with her mind! He even says it's her speciality!

She caused constant mayhem for her maternal extended family when they tried to take her back! Lights going on and off by themselves! Phones ringing off the hook! Plates moving unaided across the table! A flying doll and a trashed room!

Clive remembered Ryan actually telling him that Roxanne did not care for Carlton, or *Celestial Bodies*, and that she had gone upstairs to her bedroom to view another programme on her portable television that same night.

Oh my God! But why would she want to harm Carlton? Has she picked up on Randal's intense dislike of him? Was it to impress him at how far she has come with her inheritance? Randal loathes the fact that Carlton possesses 'the gift'. Does Roxanne feel the same way?

Surely Randal would not stoop that low by letting her effect such a diabolical achievement, without supervision? Or is it possible she did it without his knowledge in order to gain his respect? It's unthinkable but still conceivable!

Clive had to know, and he had to know right away, so he phoned Randal.

"Hello, Roxanne here. If you're another bad man wanting my daddy, I'll get very upset," she answered emphatically.

"It's your Uncle Clive here, poppet. Would you put your daddy on the phone for me, please?" he requested in a soft tone so as not to arouse her suspicion.

"Of course, Uncle Clive. He's in the kitchen making me a drink. Oh, wait, he's here now," she acknowledged, as Randal waltzed into the room with his famous chocolate milkshake.

"It's for you, Daddy. It's Uncle Clive."

"And this is for you, madam," spoke Randal in a subservient manner, and she giggled as she took her drink, then went back to her writing desk in the other room.

"Hello, you. How goes it with the nonstop inquisition?" quipped Randal, but his sarcasm was aimed at the gutter press and not at his dearest friend.

"They're driving me nuts. It's bloody endless. But that's not why I've rang. Randal, there's something I've got to know. It's bugging me and I really need to know if it's true."

"Fire away." *More questions. Am I ever going to be free of them?*

"Just tell me the absolute truth for once. Did Roxanne cause

Carlton's so-called accident?"

Randal shrank back metaphorically into the hidden shadows of the room. He was not expecting such an outright enquiry, even with all his psychic ability. The continuing silence spoke volumes and Clive's heart began to race.

"She did, didn't she?" whispered Clive, for fear of inciting Randal's wrath, Roxanne's guilt and his own desolation.

"I didn't know. At the time when it happened, I really didn't know," admitted Randal, feeling there was no point in lying to their protector.

"So… when? When did you realise?"

"Right at the very end. After I went back into the studio with you to evaluate the damage and to calm everyone down. I phoned Alison because I knew they'd all be watching the programme at home and would have seen the incident. I asked after the kids. She told me that Roxanne had decided to go to her bedroom because she didn't like Carlton, or the show. *That's* when I knew. I got a mental flash of her eyes transfixed to that blasted mount and screen. I swear to you, Clive, that I had no idea she was going to do it. Hand on heart. I'd have stopped her because the concentration was intense and it could have drained her. Damaged her, even. And that's the whole truth of the matter."

"What about Carlton? You obviously don't care about his welfare, or life-threatening injury?" admonished Clive.

"Believe it or not, I do," lied Randal. "I never liked him, but I wouldn't have used my powers to do that."

"Maybe not that, but it would have been something else, somewhere else. I know you, Randal. I know that he pushed all of your competitive buttons, simply by having the same capabilities but using them in a righteous way. Obviously, Roxanne felt the same. So, you're not really that bothered about him. It's more to do with the repercussions of his infirmity."

"That's true to a degree, but like I said, I wasn't responsible for this particular intrusive predicament we all find ourselves in."

"I see."

"Do you? Do you really see, Clive?"

"I close my mind to what I don't want to see."

"Clive, you know what I am, who I am. Roxanne as well. What we both are. You know that 'the gift' is far greater than any of us. There are times when it becomes all-consuming. We have to stretch its primeval legs."

"But you could do so much good! You could achieve so much more! The world needs you, Randal. It needs your genius, your amazing legacy. It doesn't need your destructive goals."

"You sound like Carlton."

"I'm not even thinking about Carlton and the way he feels. This is me! This is what I feel. This is your protector who wants to keep you safe."

"Look, Clive, I don't think you realise how hard I've tried to dumb it all down for you. Roxanne has as well. We care about you and don't want a repetition of your desperate state, that terrible day when we thought you'd left us. That taught us to conceal any further harmful situations, even though your role is written. You know it's engraved, Clive, in a sacred doctrine, from the beginning of our earthly connection; from the start of the many lifetimes we've been together," endorsed Randal, his nostrils flaring with imperious passion.

"I understand, but I don't approve. I'll never leave you both and I'll always be loyal and remain silent."

"We know that, Clive. I nearly lost you and that's when it really sunk in. How much I care. How much I need you. How much I love you. In as much as I can ever care, need or love."

Clive nodded. His love for Randal was immortal. Whatever transpired in the name of 'the gift' would have to be buried inside the joyless corners of his guilty contemplation.

"I love you, Randal. I always will."

"Ditto. I'll see you tomorrow. OK?"

"I'll be waiting." *Waiting for you. Wherever you are. True to the end. God help me.*

★★★

Dean Gibson felt extremely glum, so low that all his enthusiasm for his job as controller of programmes at Astral TV had taken a visionary sabbatical. He was utterly guilt-ridden.

"I can't get Carlton out of my head," groaned Dean.

"Life goes on, Dean, and we've got to carry on regardless of this unjust intrusion," encouraged Randal. "You've worked so damn hard on future projects. You simply can't abandon them because of this unforeseen madness."

"But if it wasn't for me, and my stylish extravaganza of that astrological, one-off setting, namely the monster, unstable monitor, then none of this would be happening! Carlton would be in one piece, and Astral TV wouldn't wake up in the papers with our names emblazoned across the pages. Every day we hit the news in some way or other. Crowds of paparazzi are outside the studio, the hospital, your house and mine. It's a mess. It's as if they can't wait for Carlton to die and lay the blame at our door," he groaned.

"Dean. Dean, look at me," urged Randal.

"It's a bloody wonder you can look at me at all. I've let you down so badly."

Randal put his arm around Dean's shoulder. "Now listen to what I have to say and pay attention to each word. Stop wallowing in negativity and blame. What happened to Carlton was out of our hands. Some bonehead engineer messed up big-time. His expertise was in defective, short supply. Techscreen are the guilty party, not your unique studio set. Your intentions were honourable. Fate played a cruel trick by bringing in a company who commissioned deficient labour," stressed Randal.

"But I picked the company!"

"But you didn't pick the engineer! You didn't choose him personally. They employed him and they're at fault. It was their shortcoming, their misdeed and their demerit that caused the disaster. Any jury will see that we're blameless. Techscreen are trying their best to blacken and malign our reputation, to disguise their own incompetence. They're basing their case upon sabotage. It'll be thrown out of court."

"Spencer doesn't think so! What's got up his snooty nose? He's out to get you, Randal. He's always been so jealous of your success. It's as if he's grabbed this chance to totally discredit you, to pull you down to his underhanded level. Some bloody cousin he's turned out to be!"

Randal's eyes began to burn and the yellow glints glittered with curbed malice. He walked away from Dean and turned his back on him, just in time, as his vision became illuminated, radiating with freakish light. He took a very deep breath and used his powers to stop the uncontrollable rage that was running riot through his veins at the mention of Spencer's name.

Dean mistook Randal's reaction for humiliation. "Randal, I'm so sorry. I didn't mean to rub it in. Spencer's your dad's family, after all. He's a Forbes. I'm your dear mother's side, and my mum's her treasured younger sister, and they're very, very close. I've no right to call your dad's side, but this vindictiveness is causing a split. I hate it."

"There'll be no split," affirmed Randal, turning round to face Dean again.

"But your mum's absolutely furious with Spencer! I know it's going to explode and I don't think I can cope with both families at each other's throats."

"You won't have to. I'm sure of that."

"How sure? Spencer's prosecuting us. It's so disloyal. Detestable!"

"Spencer's totally off his trolley. He went AWOL a year or so ago. He hid himself away like some demented monk and wouldn't speak to anyone, not even his own parents or brother."

"Why?"

"Fuck knows. But I do know that his father, my Uncle Ashley, fears for Spencer's sanity. He's going to approach his chambers and tell them he's too unstable to represent Techscreen. So, they are going to have to find another barrister. One that who won't be so obsessed with discrediting us. We've nothing to worry about, Dean."

"Carlton's my worry. He's the victim in all of this. We became close and I really like him. Now his family are after my blood. They blame me totally because he would still be a well-known astrologer, just writing his newspaper columns and broadcasting his radio programmes, without my grand idea that propelled him to national stardom. It's my fault. All my fault."

Randal felt the stirrings of 'the gift' surface yet again.

Won't this blasted starman ever disappear up his own birth chart and get astrologically stuffed!

"Dean, Dean, Dean! Carlton may still recover. Don't give up on him. Clive came out of his coma against all the odds, still intact, without brain damage. You've got to have faith. But in the meantime, I want you to carry on with your impressive workload. Astral TV needs you. I need you. Is that clear enough?"

"I'll try."

"And you'll succeed, like you always have! Look what you've been through in your early years, Dean. Far worse than this unfortunate incident. Believe me, it will all go away and things will work out for us. I'll make sure of that."

"I believe you, just like I've always believed in you," acknowledged Dean, with a worshipful look on his handsome face.

"Then let's make programmes. Huh?"

"I guess. You're the boss."

"Of course, I am." Randal smiled, but inside he was seething.

I didn't remove your useless father and half-brother for nothing. They were totally redundant in your life. You belong with me at the top of your gifted tree. I'll protect you from lesser mortal, bad blood. I always have and I always will.

So, look out, flea-bitten Flint! And that goes for you too, splenetic Spencer. I'm the autonomous auctioneer. I give you all fair warning.

Going, going, gone!

2

The Daily Announcer
Tuesday 10th March 1992

ASTRAL TV WIN SUBSTANCIAL DAMAGES AGAINST
TECHSCREEN!
RANDAL FORBES' COMPANY DECLARED
INNOCENT OF ALL CHARGES!

Astral TV have been found not guilty of spurious sabotage! Astrologer and celebrity Carlton Flint, 41, was seriously injured by a falling suspended mount, and its attached monitor, which crashed down on his head last September, causing his ongoing comatose state.

Astral TV owner, and an author and entrepreneur, Randal Forbes, 34, and his cousin, Dean Gibson, 26, who is controller of programmes, were both exonerated from all charges.

Techscreen, who, in turn, were countersuing Forbes and Gibson, lost their case and were ordered to award the sum of half a million pounds in damages to Carlton Flint and his family. Also, one hundred thousand pounds was awarded to Forbes and Gibson for damaged reputations, and five thousand pounds each to the two claimants, who retained injured limbs in the crush to exit the studio on the night.

The barrister Spencer Forbes, 33, Randal Forbes' cousin, who was originally representing Techscreen, was dismissed before the court proceedings.

His father, Ashley Forbes, 59, effected his termination.

As a character witness for the plaintiffs, he informed all involved of his son's serious mental health issues and felt he was not of sound mind to conduct a balanced case. He stated the following:

"It would have been grossly unfair to both the plaintiffs and the defendants, in this complicated lawsuit, if my son was still representing the prosecution. He has a serious depressive, stress-related illness, and should not be allowed to influence the verdict as a result."

Crucially, a neutral inspection of the site showed that Techscreen did not take into consideration the concrete ceiling and failed to drill the holes deep enough to accommodate the bolts and screws to ensure the stability of the mount.

Additional anchors were also found to be unstable.

The jury found Techscreen totally liable, beyond any reasonable doubt, for a defective and dangerous installation.

Randal Forbes gave *The Announcer* the following statement after the verdict:

"On behalf of myself, Dean Gibson and all at Astral TV, I wish to thank our legal team for their tireless work in this case. We are enormously relieved that we have been absolved of this bogus and erroneous accusation. It was a crass, spiteful censure on Techscreen's part, to shift the blame to my company and damage our trustworthy reputation.

"Having said all that, let's not forget the critically injured Carlton Flint and his family. We all pray for his recovery over time and send our sincere good wishes to each and every one of them.

"With respect to my cousin, Spencer Forbes, who was taken off the struggling on a daily basis with a severe mental disorder, I entment.

"His previous stance against my company was borne out of his illness. He is most unfit and traumatised.

"We all wish him well, and very much hope that in time, normality and civility will be fully restored."

★★★

Carlton Flint was constantly dreaming. At least he thought he was. He had blacked out but could still hear his wife's distinctive, caring voice.

"I'm losing faith, Dr Ramsey," sighed Francine. "He's been in this coma for months now. Will he ever wake up, and even if he does, will he be brain-damaged and still on life support?"

Carlton needed to blink, but his eyelids were frozen. His head felt as heavy as a lump of rock, but he recognised Francine's speech. Who was the doctor she was talking to? Was he sleeping, or in some kind of parallel universe? His dreams were never-ending, but recently they had taken a more realistic turn. Whereas before they were primarily visual, now they were also audible, and constantly featured Francine, and the same medic.

"I'm still cautiously optimistic, Mrs Flint. There are some good signs, just a few, but enough to be encouraging."

"Really?"

"Yes. We have to stay positive."

Carlton tried to make sense of their words. Then it all clicked into place! He was in hospital in a comatose state. A psychic flash of a large, square object blazed into his fragile subconscious. A screen with multi-coloured lights twinkling in the darkness. Suspended but dangerous. Then, two slate-grey eyes, with flashing yellow glints, sliced through the gloom, and the screws and bolts turned deliberately under the strict telepathic command of the deadly, lustrous gaze.

The mount shifted, the screen swayed from side to side, and then it crashed down on his head. His brain was badly damaged but there was still a part of it that functioned psychically, of that he was certain. And now, another realisation! An infernal force had tried to kill him but had failed!

The eyes were those of a little girl. A beautiful but unrighteous, darkly educated, striking child, caught up in the heretical spirit of her father's ungodly disposition. She was guilty but innocent. Culpable but blameless. Single-minded but influenced. Carlton scanned his remaining functioning braincells to pull out the names of his violators.

"You must be so relieved that the court case is over and that Techscreen were found guilty," affirmed Dr Ramsey to Francine.

"Oh, for sure. At the beginning we were all so tortured. We lashed out at the wrong people. Now we're so glad to be on talking terms again with Dean and Randal. It's been traumatic and we were grossly mistaken, laying the blame at the wrong door," she concluded, and Carlton mentally winced.

No! No, Francine! You weren't mistaken! Randal didn't do it, but his daughter did! But he may as well have! And now I must wake up because I need to stop him sinning and winning, wherever I can. I'm on my way back home with a return ticket from anaesthetised hell. So, pay attention. Yes, you! You, over there, in your treacherous corner! Randal Forbes! Stealer of souls!

***

Hadleigh Masterson had just been promoted to editor of the *Daily Announcer*. It was an advancement of great worth, especially as he was the youngest candidate after the position. His quick-fire brain and endless enthusiasm for local, national and international affairs gave him a winning-head start. He was twenty-nine, of medium height, with hazel eyes and dark brown hair. He had a cheeky, appealing smile when he turned on the charm, which was often.

"A total smartarse!" criticised a fellow journalist behind his back, but it was just sour grapes on his behalf.

Hadleigh was fascinated by Randal. He had been a fan for many years and had actually crossed paths with him fleetingly at Beaumont College, Oxford, where he was also studying English Literature. He had just begun his own course as Randal reached his third term, so he was not part and parcel of the Forbes circle.

He was also an admirer of Alison's music. His fiancée, Tanya, had purchased two tickets for the last ill-fated performance of *Priestess*. They were both there to witness Maxine's spectacular, fatal plunge down the theatrical stairway. As tragic as that was, he still played the soundtrack of songs from the show on a regular basis. Alison's music moved him, and Randal's lyrics spoke to his spirit.

Randal was always in the news. Hadleigh had written a piece about Clive, namely his extraordinary recovery and Randal's close proximity to the event. He recalled the consultant physician's comments, stating that Clive's revival was almost supernatural, a mysterious one-off restoration, unlike anything he had ever witnessed in his whole medical career.

More recently, Hadleigh had followed the Carlton Flint case, both in and out of court, resulting in Astral TV's emphatic vindication. Yet again, Randal was smack in the middle of all the complex legalities and injurious, dark chain of events.

He had the feeling that Randal was very 'other'. It shone throughout all his literary work and was very evident in his whole demeanour and creative essence.

Retrospectively, he recalled a great number of students in Oxford, crowding round Randal in worshipping droves, with Clive conjoin-twinned to his side, like some unpaid valet. It seemed that Clive had remained in the same obedient position, albeit that of his agent and PA, but still subservient and eternally attentive.

Hadleigh was intent on his paper covering an in-depth article on Randal's whole career, right back to his childhood days. He wanted to publish it in their glossy Sunday magazine supplement. Normally he would send another journalist to cover the story. But not this one. He wanted to be the interviewer, to get really close to the captivating source. The spell-binding, transfixing presence of a modern-day celebrity. The multi-talented, enigmatic Randal Forbes, who still exuded a paradoxical air of masculine and androgynous authority. He thought about it long and hard.

I'd prefer to conduct the interview in his family setting, but I know that Randal's fiercely private and protective of his wife and children. Still, it's worth a try even though most of his recent press has been intrusive. My paper has tried to remain impartial throughout the whole court proceedings, which is a huge plus. We've showed far more integrity than some of our fellow journals. Randal despises media intrusion, so I'll have to play it very cautiously and tone down the numerous questions I'm itching to ask him. Fingers crossed!

Hadleigh had access to Clive's business number. He made the call but the line was engaged. After several more attempts he was successful.

"Hello, Clive Hargreaves, can I help you?"

"You certainly can! My name's Hadleigh Masterson and I'm the editor of the *Daily Announcer.*"

"I'm sorry, but Mr Forbes is adamant there will be no more interviews about the recent court case. It's all done and dusted," intercepted Clive.

"Oh, no! I'm not ringing about that! I'd like to interview Mr Forbes about his whole career. I was actually at Beaumont College with you both, only you were in your final year as I began my first term," he said in the hope of buttering Clive up.

"Oh, I see. With respect, I don't remember you. However, Mr Forbes will not want to be interviewed. He's most particular about who he sees, and he definitely doesn't want any further intrusion."

"I totally get that, but this would be a very complimentary and principled account of his influence and diverse talents. I don't wish to sound sycophantic, but I'm a great admirer. I'd consider it an honour if he were to accept my proposal. Can't you at least test the water? If he refuses, then I'll obviously back off, but tell him it will all be above-board, with no hidden agenda. Just a comprehensive article about his past and present success and effect."

"Hmm. Well, I guess I can ask him, but don't hold your breath."

"Oh, that's fine. That's more than fine. Should I ring again, or what?"

"No, I'll phone you back, either way," acknowledged Clive. "What's your direct number?"

"Thank you so much for your valuable time," replied an elated Hadleigh, as he gave Clive his contact details.

★★★

The next day, Clive told Randal about Hadleigh's call, and he was both surprised and slightly startled by his response.

"Hadleigh Masterson? Nope, I don't remember him, but he must have been a bright spark to get Beaumont. I like his name. It's got a cool ring to it. You know something, Clive, I've had a bucketful of crappy publicity. It'll be good to have a true follower on board. Give him a bell. No, wait! What's his number? I'll call him personally."

Clive felt more than a bit put out. It was Randal's readiness to embrace a new admirer that rattled his cage by proxy. Up until now, he had been relentless in his disdain of all journalists alike. Suddenly, and unexpectedly, he wanted to actually meet one of the detractors.

"Be very careful, Randal. You don't really know this guy," insisted Clive.

"I know that he wants to put me on a pedestal. So why not? It's where I belong!"

***

On the 31st March 1992, Carlton finally pulled himself out of his hellish hibernation and woke up. His eyes rolled behind their lids, stuck fast inside their sockets. With a determination born out of a combative realisation of his whereabouts and present condition, he literally willed himself awake.

That's it. Now move your eyes. Take your time. To the left, right, look ahead, look around. Slowly does it.

Then, with self-discipline of supernatural proportions, he opened and closed his mouth, licking his dry, cracked lips. Next, he flexed his fingers on both hands, scrunching the digits in and out of a stiff but promising movement. His limbs were a different story. Months of inertia had caused muscle loss.

It doesn't matter. My powers will make them strong again.

He located a buzzer at the side of his bed, the one for the nurse. He concentrated hard but could not stretch out to use it.

Use your mind. You can do it.

He closed his eyes and focused hard. The buzzer rang out.

That's it. You're getting there.

Winston was at the front desk when the bell sounded. His head spun round to acknowledge the call because it was rare that a patient on life support would be able to press it. He ran over to Carlton, whose eyes were wide open and blinking.

He paged the neurologist as he pulled up a chair at Carlton's bedside. He shone a light in both of his eyes. "Can you understand me, Mr Flint? If you can, blink twice."

Carlton responded but needed the tube down his throat to be removed immediately before any more communication.

"Do you know where you are? Don't be afraid. You're in hospital and you've been unconscious."

Carlton half-smiled and spoke to Winston telepathically, because he had no other choice.

32

Please, please take this tube out. The one that's down my throat. I don't need it anymore.

Winston's eyes became two, huge, round saucers of disbelief. Surely that was not Carlton Flint's voice he had just heard inside his head?

Dr Ramsey, please don't be alarmed. It's the only way I can communicate with you at the moment, until my damaged brain repairs itself. I know you find it hard to believe, but please take the tube away.

Winston's heart leaped out of his chest as Carlton's request hit home. "Oh! What's happening here? How do you know my name? This is unbelievable!" exclaimed Winston, as he removed the offending tube.

Carlton made a gurgling noise. He licked his dry lips again; they felt chapped and dehydrated. At that same moment, the neurologist Dr Jack Roseland walked into the room.

"He's awake, Jack. Awake and aware," said Winston to his fellow medic, still in a daze over the telepathic communication.

"Are you sure?"

"I'm sure, see for yourself."

Dr Roseland looked at Carlton, who stared back at him resolutely and even managed another half-smile.

"Well, well, well. A breakthrough at last, but let's be cautious and not jump the gun."

"I've not contacted his wife yet, but I think we should."

"By all means, but play it down in case he loses consciousness again. We don't want his family to have false hope. It's far too early, but I'm delighted that he's woken up. That's a massive plus in itself."

Please! Phone Francine and tell her I'm going to be OK. It'll take time, and when I'm well enough, I'll explain everything to you, Dr Ramsey.

Winston's head jerked backwards and his heart skipped another beat. Again! Something very strange was happening. Was it just him or had Jack Roseland heard the same request?

No, he can't hear me. I'm just communicating with you because I know you have an open mind. You don't dismiss telepathy as easily as your colleagues do. So, you'll be my main contact and I don't want you to discuss it.

Winston looked into Carlton's eyes and nodded in affirmation. He was incredibly excited by the enormity of the whole extraordinary situation. Carlton's awakening by telepathic means was just spine-tingling! If he could converse in this way and pick up thoughts, then he had powers: a capability that most people did not possess.

Then suddenly, for no reason, Randal's face fired into Winston's memory banks. Only recently, Clive Hargreaves was in this intensive care unit. In the very same bed that Carlton Flint now occupied. That situation was so off the wall it was dangling in the psychic street. Something was telling him that Carlton and Randal had been hatched out of the same alien egg. The body snatchers from Planet Earth, with a twist of undecipherable significance to put him off the true scent.

Firstly, his immediate priority lay with Carlton's recovery. If he could communicate telepathically then maybe he could effectuate his own healing process? That would be something to behold. Winston would give him a conventional helping hand, but he could not contain his excitement in seeing the spiritual remedy unfold and astound.

★★★

Spencer was knocking back his third glass of wine when the news of Carlton's awakening was announced on the radio. The liquid went down the wrong way, and he coughed and spluttered, spraying the front of his white polo shirt with crimson blobs. The report was very positive and the prognosis encouraging.

It was the first time in weeks that Spencer felt half alive. *Is this the start of a new dawn?*

In all of the time that Carlton had been unconscious, Spencer could not pluck up the courage to visit him in hospital or even contact his family. His father, Ashley Forbes, had made the nightmarish situation so much worse by telling Spencer's superiors that he was mentally unfit to represent his clients. As a result, he had been laid off work indefinitely, and his legal career was hanging precariously in the balance.

Spencer was incandescent with anger because he now felt that Randal, or Roxanne, or both of them, were guilty of the complicated, deadly, unsavoury performance that had left Carlton clinging on by his comatose fingertips. Now, thanks to Spencer's meddling father, nobody in authority would ever believe him.

He only had one single ally. Carlton! Hopefully, with a lot of tender loving care, he would once again have his protector and loyal supporter seeking justice in his fighting corner.

Randal had already sweet-talked his way back into the confidence and favour of the Flint family. When Spencer read his comments in the *Daily Announcer*, after the case was dropped against Astral TV, who had won a hefty sum in damages, he actually burst into tears.

It would have been better if he had felt furious and broken every plate in his kitchen cupboard, but he had reached a point of overwhelming sorrow at his unjust plight and Randal's hypocritical, cunning get-well wishes for him, and everyone else involved.

He knew he would never win. He could not expose his false-hearted cousin as a cold-blooded, vile murderer. Inspectors Leonard Galloway and Ronald Grey had both suspected and could not prove a thing. They were both exterminated just in case they hit upon a judicial clue of Randal's absolute involvement with a solid substantiation.

But now, Carlton's making a spectacular comeback! The one person who not only believes my accusations, but who actually possesses the

*telepathic powers and psychic ability to move mystical mountains. For the
good. For the honourable. For the righteous. Randal's fiercest opposition.
Yes!*

The telephone began to ring as the news bulletin ended.

"Hello, can I help you?" asked Spencer, with a wide grin on
his face.

It was his father, Ashley Forbes.

"Spencer, it's me."

There was no reply. Just complete silence.

"Spencer, don't put down the phone!" begged Ashley. "Your
mother wants to speak to you. I know you won't talk to me, but
I had to do what I did for all the right reasons. One day you'll
see that I was only thinking of your welfare."

"Dad, please! All of you! Leave me alone! You don't believe
a word I say, and you don't understand the gravity of the whole
situation!"

Just as he was about to hang up, his mother, Julia, intervened.
"Spencer, darling. I'm so desperately worried about you. Come
back to Didsbury and stay with us, just for a little while, and
make a clean break away from all of this… this imagined danger.
Just come home and get help."

"Mum, I know you're upset, but I can't come back. Dad sees
Uncle Edward all the time and I wouldn't be able to keep my
mouth shut about Randal. His beloved, despotic, despicable,
demonic-eyed son."

"But that's the reason we want you here with us, so that
we can get to the root of all the trouble. Your Uncle Edward
doesn't know what you've actually said about Randal. He just
believes you're both estranged. He's far from happy when you
wanted to represent Techscreen, as is your Aunty Margaret,
but since the verdict, we've managed to smooth things over by
telling them… well, by explaining you're… you're…"

"Mad? Is that you what you mean, Mum?"

"Oh, God, no! No, Spencer! You're just unwell."

"Well, funnily enough, today I feel alive and kicking. Someone who actually believes in me and my 'madness' is now back in my corner."

"Who?"

"Carlton Flint."

"But he's in a coma."

"Not anymore. He's awake. It's on the news."

"I don't understand. He's Randal's connection. He made him a star. Randal's on good terms with the Flint family now. So why would Carlton think badly of him?"

"Because he knows what he really is, and he detests him and everything he stands for."

Julia sighed deeply. "This is *exactly* what I mean by you needing to come back home."

"No, Mum. What I need is poetic justice. Randal's always banging on about that. I assure you he will not be happy that Carlton is conscious. Neither will Roxanne."

"Roxanne? What's she got to do with it?"

"She's Randal's daughter and has inherited all his demonism."

"What! She's adopted! Now you're talking double nonsense! Oh, Spencer!"

"She's his blood child! His and Maxine's! That's why he killed Maxine, and then Saul, so he could claim her back! I know you don't believe me. If I were you, I wouldn't believe me, but *everything* I've told you and Dad is the truth, the whole truth and nothing but the truth! I'm not ill. I'm just telling you how it is – something I should have done a long time ago. I've known this since we were children. He was always evil. *Always!* He's fooled you all. Every single one of you!"

Julia bit her bottom lip so hard it began to bleed. Her son was breaking her heart into little pieces. She desperately needed him to come home. To keep an eye on his fragile state. *Oh, God help him.*

Julia took a deep breath then spoke aloud in a gentle tone. "I believe that you believe what you're telling me, darling, but if you come home, we could talk about every little thing on your mind and try to work it all out together as a family," she urged.

"What you mean is for me to see a shrink, preferably in close proximity to you and Dad, so you can all exorcise the demon out of my damaged head. Well, it's not going to happen! I'm staying put with Carlton Flint by my side! You'll see! You'll all see that I'm not mad when he verifies every single word I've said!" snorted Spencer, with more than a touch of his old insufferable self.

He was back in his supercilious front row seat as he slammed down the phone on his mother.

They just don't get it! Just wait until Carlton's firing on all cylinders! Randal, he's coming to get you, so look out! Your reign will soon be over!

★★★

Twenty-four hours after Spencer had told his parents where to get off, he had the most uncontrollable urge to go for an early-morning run. He changed into his designer sportswear. The same outfit he had purchased to impress his snooty ex-fiancée, who would not entertain anyone in high-street clothes. He felt energised and whistled a popular tune as he sprinted down the street. He could not remember the last time he felt so carefree, and his thoughts reflected that liberation.

Sod the lawsuits and two fingers up to the establishment!

He ran across the busy road, ignoring all the cars. He scampered in and out of the rush-hour traffic, avoiding bumpers and laughing out loud as he dodged yet another irate motorist.

"Up yours, too!" he shouted to the driver of a silver Honda, who let rip with a stream of obscenities as he nearly ran him over.

"Look at me! I'm amazing! I'm untouchable! I'm fucking immortal!"

He raced back along the edge of the road, and two lanes of traffic whizzed by him, honking their horns.

"Oh yeah!" he yelled. "What a buzz!"

He changed direction again and then sprinted along the walkway of the bridge that spanned the motorway. Suddenly he stopped. Someone was calling him and he moved his head from side to side in order to decipher the words. The traffic below him was hefty, as he leaned against the concrete wall and watched the drivers beneath him.

Spencer! Hey, Spencer! Guess who?

He could not comprehend why his feet were suddenly glued to the spot and how he could hear a single, solitary voice above all the surrounding transportation. Why was he stuck in one place?

Don't you know who I am? You should. You've talked enough rot about me. Tut, tut. What a shame that nobody believes a word you say. Oh, but I do. You always were a stickler for the facts.

Spencer was confused. He wanted to carry on running, far away from the words in his head that were full of mockery and menace.

You've asked for this, you know. You just couldn't keep your foul mouth shut. Oh, I tried, Spencer. I really, really tried to leave you alone, but now you've given me no choice. So, cousin dear, climb up towards the top of the wall.

Spencer obeyed without question.

Now pull yourself up, then bend over and pretend you're going to roly-poly down a hill, like we did when we were kids. You were the most supercilious, sneaky, intolerable brat that I ever had the misfortune to taunt.

Spencer pressed down on the top of the wall with his hands. He bent forward with his head facing down and watched the cars and lorries below, moving steadily towards their different destinations.

Enjoying the view? Now I want you to roly-poly once more, at the count of three.

Spencer felt his invader pull away. Reality kicked in and he was horrified to find himself curved over a rigid, vertical structure, with a motorway beneath him. What the hell was he doing there?

You're saying goodbye. Just like Andy Pandy. That's what you're doing. Spencer is waving goodbye. Here we go then. Rock 'n' roly-poly. All fall down.

Just for a split second before he plummeted over the wall, Spencer knew exactly who had led him to this point in time. *Randal!*

The driver of an ice-blue Mercedes shrank back in horror behind the wheel, as Spencer's falling body smashed against his windscreen and bounced off the bonnet into the road, only to be run over by another set of wheels. Then the vehicle behind slammed into him, creating a domino effect of colliding cars, a multiple pile-up of unmitigated disaster with Spencer at the helm, fatally flattened in the middle of the road, with several other victims inside their husks of crushed metal.

For his own safety, Randal had pulled out of Spencer's head before he hit the ground.

Shucks, what a pity I couldn't see it happen, but it'll be on the national news for sure. More intrusive press possibly knocking at my door. But hey ho. Mission accomplished. Quick and slick.

His eyes stopped glowing as he put Spencer's photograph back into the family album. His mouth curled upwards in a cruel, dispassionate line. He nodded, brushed back his damp hair, then walked into the main room with a military bearing.

"You started writing early," said Alison. "I didn't want to disturb you."

"I've just written one of my best scenes. It's kind of emotional because the character met an untimely end. But it had to be done. Shame. Now what's for breakfast?"

★★★

40

One week later, Roxanne dipped her toasted soldiers into the softly boiled egg, oblivious to any grief. Ryan and Amber followed suit, but their sad, pinched faces were tugging at Alison's heartstrings.

"I don't want the kids at the actual funeral," she whispered to Randal, "especially Roxanne. She's had enough sorrow in her short life."

"We'll travel down to my parents' house and they can all stay there with one of the adults. Victoria, my ever-faithful nanny, will probably remain behind and look after them."

Alison nodded. Roxanne looked over at Randal as she licked the runny egg around her bottom lip. Their modulated voices did not fool her. She knew exactly what had happened. Spencer had been gossiping about Randal's powers, and he would have spoiled everything if allowed to carry on in the same way.

Spencer was another bad man. Just like the starman but without 'the gift'.

Randal picked up on her thoughts and spoke to her mind. *That's true, pumpkin. He went too far.*

I know, Daddy. I wish I could have done it with you, but you didn't ask me. Why?

It was easier to do it quickly on my own. It was simple.

I understand. But you know I'll always help if I can. I'm a good girl, really.

A very good girl. Now eat up and then we'll get ready to drive down to Didsbury.

When we get there, I'll look upset.

No need to.

Oh, but I will. Just like this.

Roxanne stopped chewing and scrunched up her face into a grievous expression. She began to sob and the tears cascaded down her face on cue.

Ryan put his arm around her shoulder. "Don't cry, Roxanne. Please don't cry. We're all upset about Spencer," he soothed.

Then Amber burst into tears of misplaced commiseration, and Ryan turned to comfort her as well. Alison then consoled the disturbed trio.

As much as he didn't like to see them all distressed, Randal's mouth twitched with hidden black humour. What a pantomime his chosen child had created. He would be really glad when it was all over. He was not looking forward to seeing his Uncle Ashley and Aunty Julia wrapped up in a cloak of grief and anguish.

Don't worry, Daddy. They all thought Spencer was mad. They didn't believe him about 'the gift' so we're both safe. But I'm still very upset about the starman waking up. He's much more of a bad man than Spencer was. What are we going to do about him?

Randal looked directly at Roxanne. She was such a good actress, looking for the entire world like a bereaved child but all the time communicating telepathically with him. A chip off the old bewitching block. What a class act.

Forget about the starman for now. He's still not properly awake and he's far from well.

But he could get better.

He might, but we'll think of something again if he does.

Something?

Yes, something. Anything to stop him stopping us.

I love you, Daddy.

I know. Now finish your breakfast. Use your napkin, pumpkin; you've got egg on your face.

So has the starman.

It took Randal all of his time not to laugh out loud at his precocious, precious daughter. Head bowed at her advanced altar! Roxanne knew she was Randal's favourite child. Uncle Clive's, too.

Daddy, what will you tell Uncle Clive? He's just got back from Italy. I don't want him ill again.

Randal heard her concern for Clive's welfare.

He might be coming to the funeral, but I'll make sure he's OK.
Does he know it was you who made Spencer fall over the wall?
He suspects, but I'll get round him.
Suspects?
He probably thinks it could be me. Don't worry because I'll make
sure he believes it was just Spencer's illness, that he couldn't cope, so he
jumped.
That's good.

Roxanne nodded and looked deeply into Randal's eyes. It was like peering into a mirror. He smiled at her. His special smile. Her heart flipped and tripped with love for him. There was not one other person in the universe who she loved as deeply as him. Not even Clive, who came a close second. As far as she was concerned, Randal could press the nuclear button and she would still be worshipping at his atomic shrine.

Everything she thought, tried or did was to attract his attention. She craved his ultimate approval and admiration. She lived just to please and praise him.

Randal had saved her from the jaws of implacable boredom. Roxanne's maternal grandparents, and the rest of that pointless family of prevailing small-fry, filled her with dismay and disdain. A millennium would not be enough time in between visits. She studied her unparalleled father. He was just breath-taking: physically, mentally, psychically and creatively. She knew that he had heard her adulatory thoughts, but she wanted him to. She needed him to.

Amber stated to cry again. Alison was having trouble stopping her, so Roxanne zoomed in on her sister's plight and wanted to console her.

"Amber, don't be sad. I've worked it out. Spencer was poorly and now he's asleep. He won't be upset anymore. So, let's all be glad that he's better now," she purred, holding her hand.

Roxanne felt the power build up in her mind and her touch became hot and healing. Amber stopped weeping and hugged her. She felt a warm, uplifting glow throughout her whole body from Roxanne's touch, and now she was feeling calm and accepting of the situation.

"You're the best sister ever. I'm so glad you're here with me," said Amber lovingly.

"That's what sisters are for. I'm a good girl, really."

Once again, Ryan was caught up in Roxanne's fascinating and overpowering presence. He had stopped trying to analyse her mind-reading act. She had bewitched them all. In fact, he could not remember a time when she was not there. It was as if a red-haired fairy had sprinkled magic dust over their family circle and had arrived to put everything right. She always knew exactly what to say or do.

Daddy, Ryan thinks I'm Mary Poppins.

With an umbrella or a broomstick?

Alison interrupted their mental jesting. "I think we better make tracks now. Let's tidy up and get going, Randal. It's a long drive."

"Your mum's right, so come on, kids, get your skates on."

"I've not finished my toast," complained Roxanne.

"Then take it with you," suggested Randal.

"I hate cold toast."

"I'll breathe on it," he quipped.

Ryan and Amber laughed out loud, but Roxanne pulled a face.

"Come on, mini-minx. I'll make you some fresh, hot toast at Grandma Margaret's."

"I don't like the bread she buys."

"Don't you now?" teased Randal.

"Can't we take our own bread with us, Mummy? Daddy's making fun but I really, really don't like Grandma's," she pouted.

"Now why's that, my little toasted expert?" provoked Randal mercilessly.

"Because it's too thick and it makes me cough out loud."

"Oh well, in that case, we'll take a bottle of simple linctus with, just in case you get a permanent tickle at breakfast."

"I don't want to make a fuss."

"A fuss? No! Since when have you ever made a fuss? You're the most 'unfussiest' child I know," he mocked.

"There's no such word, and you're being silly now."

Randal threw back his head and laughed.

"Randal, stop teasing her. We've got a whole loaf in the breadbin, so just get it," insisted Alison.

"Oh, you demanding females," he chided with a salute.

"I'm not demanding. I'm just particular," huffed Roxanne.

Then it was Alison's turn to laugh out loud at her adult response.

Randal was more than glad of the trivial distraction because he had to pull out all the fallacious stops at the terminus of his unwanted but necessary journey. Ho hum. It was all such a drag. He could think of much better ways of spending the next few days.

Day one with Alison. In the shower. Ecstasy!

Day two with Lady Pennington. In her four-poster bed. Kinky!

Day three with Clive. In a frenzied, bisexual jamboree. Naughty!

Instead, it was going to be the Forbes family heartbreak hotel, with his mother's side also thrown in for added, grim effect. Maybe he was being too unfeeling. He should not let his cruel black humour lessen the genuine grief for his deceased but insufferable cousin.

So, chin up, shoulders back, and stiff upper lip does it! That's what Dad always taught me as a kid. To be strong, with a twist of compassion. After all, I'm still a Forbes. It's not my fault that Uncle Ashley's first-born was hellbent on destroying my character and reputation.

The ending he had provided for Spencer was in keeping with his cousin's frail mental state, so any suspicion would be eliminated and the blame would lie solely at Spencer's own suicidal door.

3

Carlton Flint was on the verge of verbal communication. He was still hospitalised but awake. He only slept when he needed to and was liaising telepathically with Winston Ramsey, every step of the progressive way.

When I'm able to talk to you openly, without struggling, I'll know that a complete recovery is on the cards. My limbs are still weak but a lot stronger than they were. It's just hard to coordinate my movements. My body won't obey my brain yet. But it will. I'm sure.

Winston was still astounded by Carlton's powers. He was astonished and highly privileged to be chosen as his receiver. At Carlton's request, he had not revealed any of their 'conversations', but however strong his leverage was, Carlton still had extensive brain damage.

Winston thought the situation was far from medically conventional, so he could expect the unexpected. The rules did not apply here. The healing goalposts had been moved to the other end of the pitch. If Carlton could speak to him telepathically, with damaged braincells, then he may have the capacity to restore them altogether.

Their transmission had been surreal, prompting Winston to tell Carlton about another startling recovery, namely Clive Hargreaves.

"I tell you, Carlton, I was there, and I saw that miracle take place right in front of me. In this very same bed. I've always thought that it was entirely due to Randal Forbes. The recovery, I mean. Clive was dying and then he was resurrected. Randal's eyes, blood pressure and whole reaction had been overwhelming. I feel he also has the power to heal. He's... how can I say? He's very daunting. His eyes are almost alien. Freakish. Quite unsettling. You know him better than me. Have you sensed his outlandish aura?"

We'll talk about that again, but right now there's something I want you to do for me because the time's right. I need complete privacy for this, so will you draw the curtains round my bed and stay with me?

"Of course," affirmed Winston, already swishing the screens.

I'm in a catch-22. I need to put my hands firmly on either side of my head, but I can't move my arms high enough and I haven't got the strength to keep them in place. I know that my brain's now ready to be healed. I had to reach a certain point, so please help me to complete the process.

Winston nodded. His heart skipped several beats as he lifted Carlton's arms up and placed his hands where he wished them to be.

Please don't go. Keep them firmly around my head. I won't harm you, but you'll feel a great surge of energy and there'll be an exact moment when you can leave me to my own recovery. Don't be alarmed by the excitation.

Carlton's hands grew very hot. Winston felt the intense heat transfer from them into his own. He watched, transfixed, as Carlton's face changed colour from pale pink to bright red.

A network of veins began to throb around his temples. His eyes rolled backwards then reappeared. A startling electric-blue brilliance, radiating with an ultra-violet, dazzling display of illumination. Winston's hands felt like they had been dipped into hot coals, as a surge of violent action shot through both arms, rocketed up to his shoulders and then made its rampant way across his chest.

But he still trusted Carlton when to stop.

His patient was sweating profusely now. The perspiration was exuberant and ran down his face and body. Winston felt his own hands slide through Carlton's, as they both struggled with incalculable and ungovernable sensations. Then, just as Winston thought he had to pull away from it all, Carlton spoke to him out loud for the first time. "Now! Let go, Winston! Let go of me!"

Carlton's breathing was heavily laboured. Winston fell back into the bedside chair and followed suit.

A halo of illustrious light wrapped itself around Carlton's head. His whole body jerked and twitched with an efficacious vibration that brought movement and life back into his dormant limbs. The bed began to shake, as his body became a mass of convulsing, trembling discomfort.

An epileptic fit on the surface but a vigorous cleansing within. And then the shaking stopped as he lay very, very still.

After a short while, his shallow breathing abated. He inhaled and exhaled normally with miraculous ease. Then he sat up on his own. He turned his head towards a shell-shocked Winston and spoke to him. "I'm OK. I'm really OK now. I can sit up. Look... I can talk. I can move. I can walk. Watch me."

Winston's mouth fell open as Carlton swung his legs round and manoeuvred himself so that his feet touched the floor. He stood up. His balance was perfect. He walked from the bed to the curtain, then back again to the bed. He did it three times with effortlessness.

Then he tested his legs further by running on the spot, like an athlete in training. He picked up a glass of water and drank it all. His coordination was faultless. His smile was so wide that it almost reached his earlobes.

"So, you see, Dr Ramsey. I'm healed and whole again. And now I need your absolute word that you'll never disclose any of this to your medical associates. I don't wish to become an object of curiosity and wonder. I was born this way and have hidden my powers well. Even from my own family. Now, I can get on with my life, but I want to thank you profusely for helping me reach this state of complete recovery."

Winston gasped. Was he dreaming? Had this actually happened? A wondrous miracle? He found his voice. "I did nothing. You healed yourself. I only watched."

"You did everything by keeping my telepathic powers alive and away from prying eyes. I chose you because I knew you'd be discreet and that you believe. That was half the battle won before it even began. Your conventional treatment was crucial. The machines and medication kept a tiny but critical part of my brain alive. The cells that enable transference of thought were still active but dormant. They hadn't died because you took care of me. I owe you, my life."

"I'm honoured, truly honoured to have played a small part in your amazing recovery process. I'm also stunned. You've turned medical science on its practical head. You have my word that your remarkable powers will never be revealed. But I need to learn more about them. Just for my own desire to understand their origin and function," expressed Winston earnestly.

"There'll be plenty of time to talk. For now, I have to let my wife and daughters know I'm back in the land of the living."

"Of course! But firstly, I must alert my colleagues to your... awakening. They'll be very shocked from a traditional standpoint. Your brain was severely damaged and highly unlikely to function normally, ever again. It's the second time that this has occurred. In this very same room and bed!"

"You mean, Clive Hargreaves? Yes, I know all about that and when it happened."

"So, you believe me when I tell you that Randal Forbes healed him? I examined him, Carlton. I knew it was supernatural. You know him better than me."

"Randal Forbes is an abominable piece of work," affirmed Carlton with a grave expression.

"But he's a healer! Like yourself. That's a good thing, isn't it?"

"He's not what he appears to be. His benevolence is very sporadic. He uses his powers in a more misappropriate way."

"I don't understand," puzzled Winston.

"It's better that you don't."

"I'm not sure if I should tell you this, but he's been in the news again; well, his family have."

"Oh?"

"His cousin, the barrister Spencer Forbes. There was a court case for compensation after your accident, and he was representing you but was dismissed for mental health reasons. His own father reported him because of his irrational behaviour."

"Spencer's not mentally ill. He's just stressed. Surely his father could see that?"

"I'm afraid you're wrong. Tragically he took his own life. He jumped off a motorway bridge into rush-hour traffic and caused several other fatalities in the process."

Carlton put his fist in his mouth and groaned. *Dear God! Poor Spencer! Randalised!*

"I'm so sorry, Carlton. I didn't realise that you knew him that well. I should never have told you so soon. You've only just recovered. How stupid of me."

Carlton reassured Winston he'd done nothing wrong. The perpetrator was a demon with red hair and satanic eyes, and now he had to do something to redress the balance. And save the world from his monstrous, endless trail of destruction.

★★★

Ashley Forbes sat near his front window staring into space. Spencer's funeral had taken place and now his family were left with the emotional fallout and devastating loss. They felt mournful and uprooted. Life would never be the same again.

He blamed himself for the whole tragic situation. If only he had left Spencer to act for Techscreen, regardless of Randal countersuing them. At least that way it would have been up to his law firm to take him off the case if they thought it necessary. But not at Ashley's request, telling them that he thought his son was unbalanced.

He had violated Spencer. He had accused him of an act of betrayal against Randal. He should have left him completely alone, whether he won or lost the case, or was dismissed before it even came to court. He should have simply bowed out.

He had blamed Spencer of instability and of talking complete nonsense. He should have been gentle and kind, not abrasive and accusatory.

Ashley had found himself looking very closely at Randal on the day of the burial. Was Spencer completely disturbed or could there possibly be some crazy element of truth attached to his wild theories? Why had he been so adamant and unyielding about Randal's so-called dark side? Surely, he could not have imagined the whole unsavoury scenario?

Spencer had worked closely alongside various police authorities on several court cases, so why would he concoct a story about Randal being constantly observed and investigated but never actually charged?

Three very disturbing facts were steadfastly revolving around Ashley's head.

The first was the long-ago episode concerning Randal's primary school and his headmistress Alice Hardman, who had jumped naked into the swimming pool and drowned. Spencer claimed that Randal had made her do it, so it had looked like suicide. But it was, in fact, a telepathic murder.

Spencer had also ended his own life by throwing himself off a wall into the path of motorway traffic. There were parallel lines of similarity.

Ashley remembered the day when Alice Hardman had visited his brother Edward, all those years ago. It was pouring, and when he'd arrived, he'd found him in a state of high agitation.

According to Edward, Alice was stark raving mad, complaining that Randal had an unsettling influence on his fellow pupils. One particular boy was found in a state of near-paralysis on the floor in the school hall and she'd blamed Randal for his traumatised condition.

She had insisted that Randal was evil and there was something exceptionally odd about his eyes. As a result, Edward and Margaret both felt he was better out of that school and had enrolled him into Redwood: a private education, which was more suited to his advanced, academic needs. That was where he'd first met Clive, and they'd struck up a lifelong friendship.

The second question mark was Roxanne. Spencer had maintained that she was actually Randal's own child, that he telepathically caused the deaths of both Maxine and Saul so that he could claim her back.

Ashley had observed her very intently after the funeral. She'd sat, for the most part, on Randal's knee, with one arm wrapped around his neck. The resemblance was startling. Why had he never noticed it before? As he'd deliberated, they both turned their heads simultaneously towards him. Identical eyes seemed to burn into his line of vision: slate-grey in colour, with sparking yellow glints. It was positively unnerving and Ashley had looked away to avoid their penetrating gaze.

The third piece of the jigsaw puzzle had been the unmistakable look of love and tenderness in Clive's eyes, as he spoke softly into Randal's ear.

Ashley had studied them purposefully. He'd watched as Clive put his hand on Randal's thigh and squeezed it, and Randal had returned the favour. Spencer had been certain that there was a long-term physical relationship between them both.

From where Ashley had been sitting this looked feasible. Or was it just close, fond, platonic friendship? He was not too sure.

But even if this shocking bisexual discovery was true, and also that Roxanne was indeed Randal's blood daughter, how could it be possible that his beloved nephew had supernatural, dark powers? It only happened in books of fiction. Things of that nature did not belong in Ashley's practical world of accountancy, where so-called paranormal activity could be explained scientifically. Ashley had shaken his head in affirmation.

Spencer had also spoken about all the murders that Randal had committed. How could he hide something as hideous and horrifying as that from his whole family? Surely, he would not be able to conceal such a trail of destruction?

Ashley came back into the present and poured himself a brandy. He looked at a family photograph on the sideboard taken at Edward's fortieth-birthday party, when the cousins were children. He walked over and picked up the frame. He traced his finger around Spencer's little face. Ashley spoke passionately to his image in his mind.

I'm so, so sorry, son. I should have been there for you. I should have sat with you and really listened to your fears. I've let you down very badly. You said you had proof, real proof that Randal was evil. I should have looked at that evidence and then made my own judgement.

I'm finding it immensely hard to believe your theory. I've always had the utmost respect and admiration for Randal, so forgive me, Spencer, but I just can't grasp this dark slant you felt he possesses. But I still should have listened. I owed you that at least. Forgive me. Please forgive me.

★★★

Back in Weybridge, Randal had felt a sudden psychic urge to monitor his Uncle Ashley's grief. He zeroed in on him and saw him crying over Spencer's demise. He felt his deep sorrow but also his confusion and suspicion.

Oh, no! Please no! Don't take after your insufferable son and be on my psychic case as well.

You're my father's respected and dearest brother. I know you're struggling with Spencer's revelations and whether he was telling the truth.

I saw you watching us: myself and Roxanne. I felt your fear as you observed us both, trying to find a clue, a sign that Spencer was bang on the money and not losing his marbles. Our eyes unnerved you, but that was our knee-jerk reaction to your puzzlement. We sensed your curiosity and smelled your sudden alarm.

Back off, Uncle Ashley! Please! I don't wish to be party to such an unthinkable removal. My father adores you. We all do.

This would be a disaster of epic proportions and true heartbreak all round. So, please, please stay away for your own survival because whenever, or wherever, 'the gift' is called into question, I have to protect its legacy, no matter what.

And even close family who stand in the line of intermeddling fire have to be eradicated as a matter of unavoidable course.

★★★

Hadleigh Masterson was in a state of unbearable excitement. He would just have to pull his professional socks up and become the self-assured journalist he had always been. But today was a first: an exclusive corker of a face-to-face conference. He had to pinch himself repeatedly. He recalled the recent phone call from his long-time favourite author and entrepreneur: the unrivalled creative genius who had actually contacted him directly.

"Hi, it's Randal Forbes here. I believe you've already spoken to my agent, Clive Hargreaves, about an interview for the *Daily Announcer*'s Sunday supplement magazine? Well, I'd like to take you up on it."

Hadleigh's heartbeat had doubled, trebled and quadrupled as he fought to remain proficient and accomplished. He had really felt like yelling out loud but managed to tone down his emotions at the connection. *Randal Forbes has phoned me! Me!*

"Well, hello there, Mr Forbes! I really didn't expect your call, but I'm over the moon that you've contacted me," he'd enthused, with just the right injection of controlled surprise.

Randal had felt Hadleigh's regulated reaction and he'd smiled to himself. "So, what exactly do you have in mind? I don't answer personal questions, but where my career is concerned, well, that's a different story, if you'll pardon the pun."

Hadleigh had found his feet. It was now or never, and he needed this interview badly. In fact, he'd been dreaming about it for many years. "Well, Mr Forbes, I'd love to go into real depth about your *whole* career – literally right from the beginning. I want to know what gave you the inspiration to become an author of great works, when and where it all began, plus the many creative and entrepreneurial peaks in between."

"Sounds OK to me. It's about time I had some good publicity. In case you've been on a space shuttle, the last three months or so have been very negative and intrusive. I'm ready for a journalistic change of heart. Talking about my creative pursuits? Well, that's come at just the right time. For both of us."

"Oh, this is great! When can we get together? I'll fall in with you."

"You can come to my house. That way we'll have the privacy I need. How does that suit?"

"That's just… just bloody amazing, quite frankly. I can't believe my luck!"

"I'll send a car for you; shall we say next Thursday at noon? Where are you situated?"

"Not too far from your London office, but I can drive over myself. It's not a problem."

"No. I prefer what I said. My driver will call for you. Just give me your full address and I'll arrange it. Oh, my wife, Alison, will also be at home so we can have lunch in the conservatory. A word of advice: absolutely no photographs of my family. Just of myself."

"Whatever you want," Hadleigh had fawned.

"What I want is less intrusion. So, count yourself lucky that I'm being so accommodating. I want an article that concentrates on my positive qualities. Not any more blatant lies from recent events."

"*The Announcer* has always been on your side. We were very supportive in reporting your recent court case. As editor, I made absolutely sure, Mr Forbes."

"I'm aware of that, Mr Masterson, and, please, call me Randal."

"I assure you... Randal... that my article will be written with the utmost deference and integrity."

"That sounds sycophantic. Skip the Uriah Heap impersonation."

"I understand, but I've been an admirer of yours since my first year at Beaumont College, Oxford. You were very respected, but unfortunately I was too young to be a part of your circle."

"Are you saying I'm too old?"

"Oh God, no!"

"What were you studying, Hadleigh?"

"English Literature."

"Same as me. Seems we have this in common, regardless of the three-year deficit."

"I really didn't mean to insult you regarding that. I'm so sorry."

"You didn't. Stop apologising. I don't like deference in sickly spades. Just find the required level of adoration."

Hadleigh had laughed out loud.

"Do you find me amusing?"

"You've got my sense of humour, Randal."

"Do you want it back? Look, just bring yourself and your sense of humour, with your pen and notebook."

"You bet!"

"I don't gamble."

"Oh, I'm so looking forward to this whole experience!"

"I'd feel the same if I were you. See you Thursday."

Hadleigh shook his head with the recollection of that sardonic but amazing phone call. A sleek, black limousine pulled up outside. A uniformed chauffeur stepped out of it and rang his intercom. This was it! His most important celebrity interview to date. Randal Forbes had invited him personally to his kingdom. Hallelujah!

★★★

Randal was simmering, just like the pan of homemade vegetable soup that Alison was cooking on her new gas hob. It was bubbling in the background as Randal's dark mood intensified.

Trust you, starman, to resurrect your holy aura! You're one powerful, pious pain in the posterior! You're a level-headed liability! You're a great, fat dollop of sanctified, consecrated immortality! How did you reverse your irreversible brain damage? You must have had help! Somebody at the hospital put your squeaky-clean hands around your scheming, swollen head, so that you could heal all of your benevolent braincells.

Who's your lesser mortal saviour? I'll find out and remove you both as effectively as the planets hover around your nauseating natal chart. I'll watch you precipitate like a falling star! You won't escape me this time! You waste of spaceman!

Alison walked in, interrupting his unsavoury thoughts. She caught the remains of his glittering vision as she joined him on the leather settee. He pulled himself out of his foul contemplation and hid his displeasure well.

"What's the matter?" she asked softly, stroking his slightly

57

flushed cheek with the side of her finger and wondering why he was sat on his own, seemingly staring into space.

"I was just thinking about you. About us. It's allowed, isn't it?" he lied, and turned his head towards her.

Alison's heart began its usual heavy drumbeat rhythm. When he had *that* look in his passionate gaze she was lost. He pulled her down next to him on the couch. His mouth left a trail of feather-light kisses on every inch of her visible satin-soft skin and beyond.

"We can't. The kids are playing upstairs," she panted, "and that editor's coming any minute now."

"He's not the only one," moaned Randal, deftly lifting up her skirt and pulling down her lace panties, as he unzipped his trousers. "This won't take long, my love."

He stroked her breasts and sucked her nipples until they were rock-hard. He entered her in a frenzy of pure love and lust, with an all-consuming passion to exorcise his frustration and fury over Carlton's maddening resurrection. His deep adoration for Alison, however, was still thriving and his senses were on fire. His thrusts became urgent and he reached his explosive peak quickly, just as the doorbell rang.

"Let it ring," he groaned, still pushing inside her and caressing her breasts at the same time. "I want to come again. Just give me five minutes."

"He'll only keep ringing," moaned Alison, as she reluctantly slid away from him.

She stood up with trembling legs and straightened her clothes. Her panties were still around her ankles and she stepped out of them as the doorbell rang once more.

"Randal, I've got to answer it, so get yourself together or else *The Announcer* will have a scoop of a photo." She giggled.

"So says the panty-free, sexy lady with shaky limbs," he teased. "Anyway, I've got nothing to hide."

"Not from where I'm looking," she said suggestively, leering at his recurring, glistening erection.

He smiled. *That smile.* Again.

"Don't! Just don't!" she warned half-heartedly, wagging her finger at him as she tottered out of the room to let their visitors in, leaving her black, lace panties behind on the floor.

Hadleigh was nervously waiting on the doorstep with his photographer. He was just about to press the bell once more when Roxanne got there before Alison. She frowned when she saw him, and her scowl worsened as she looked at the camera in his associate's hand.

"I don't want any more bad men taking pictures of my daddy," she scorned.

"Your daddy's expecting us," replied Hadleigh softly. "Is he around?"

"You'll just have to wait there while I see if that's true!" she said curtly, and shut the door in his face.

Alison appeared in the large hallway and saw Roxanne's reaction. "It's OK, sweetie, we know who he is. Go back and play with Amber, and I'll see to it," she instructed.

Roxanne shrugged her shoulders and tutted as Alison kissed her cheek. She could smell Randal's aftershave all over her.

He's making another baby with Mummy. I hope it won't have 'the gift'.

Alison reopened the door to greet Hadleigh. "I'm so sorry for that. Our daughter's highly suspicious of all journalists. Please come inside. My husband will be with you shortly," she explained courteously.

"No explanation necessary, Mrs Forbes. With all the recent unjust coverage he's had, well, it's perfectly understandable that your family are feeling distrustful. I'm here to rectify all that, I hope."

"That's a welcome change," she replied warmly, her amber eyes twinkling as she pushed her burnished, brown hair behind

59

one ear, positively glowing and throbbing in the aftermath of passion. She was moist and panty-free, still craving Randal's mouth and touch.

Randal came out into the hall holding one of Alison's earrings which had come loose after his urgent and torrid lovemaking. He gave it back to her, his eyes relaying his need for further intimacy.

I still want her badly regardless of children and visitors.

He smiled at her again as he recalled her absolute submission, but then his entertainment turned into a contemptuous statement as he spotted the photographer with his camera.

"I thought I told you, no photographs of my family, Mr Masterson!" he rebuked.

"But you said that it was OK to take some of yourself. I'm sure you did. If not, then please accept my apologies for the misunderstanding," said Hadleigh in a sincere tone.

Randal relented. The discovery of Carlton's resurrection had put him in a permanent disgruntled state.

"Hmm. Yes, I did, didn't I?"

"It's just so good of you to invite me at all. The last thing I want is for you to feel uncomfortable," expressed Hadleigh with a concerned look.

"I'm never uncomfortable. Just dissatisfied," he ridiculed.

As they made their way to the conservatory, Randal put his hand up the back of Alison's skirt and squeezed her bare bottom. His guests completely missed the suggestive act. Alison gave him a look of pure lust and promise. His erection returned and he hid it with a magazine that was lying around.

Randal sat on the armchair, the bulge in his trousers still visible but concealed behind the periodical. He signalled for Hadleigh and his colleague to settle on the couch.

He lit up a cheroot, crossed his long legs, inhaled deeply and blew out the smoke across the room. His gaze was narrow with suspicion and irritation, and he was really regretting his invitation to his house guests.

He had Carlton Flint in his deadly thoughts and required space to work out a vital plan of extermination. He also needed to screw Alison again and wanted his visitors out of the way.

"Where would you like to start?" asked Hadleigh, sensing Randal's uncooperative change of heart.

"At the beginning," derided Randal.

"I think Hadleigh would be very interested in your childhood, and how you came to write poetry at only six years of age," piped up the photographer.

"And you are?" bristled Randal.

"Oh, sorry. I'm Elvis. Elvis Ford, actually. My father was a huge fan of Mr Presley, so I'm saddled with his first name. But not the looks," he joked.

"I wholeheartedly agree," mocked Randal.

"Funnily enough, I was actually commissioned to take some shots of Graceland at the request of Priscilla Presley when I was in Memphis," he boasted, ignoring Randal's condescension.

"Priscilla Presley, eh? At Graceland, no less? This present consignment must be way down the pecking order for you, Mr Elvis Ford."

Hadleigh gave Elvis a dirty look and intervened. He spoke earnestly to Randal to pacify him. "As far as I'm concerned, this interview supersedes any done-to-death photographs of Graceland."

"Does it now? Well then, let's get started.

"Started or startled?" joked Elvis.

"Mr Masterson, if I'd wanted you to bring a comedian with you, I would have hired one. So, please tell your sidekick to say nothing. Often."

Elvis blushed. He thought that Randal was way out of order and downright rude.

"Elvis, just let me do the talking, please," requested Hadleigh. "Is that OK with your good self, Randal?"

"Your best suggestion yet, so let's begin before I lose the will to live."

Hadleigh switched on his mini tape recorder. His hands were shaking with nerves, as Alison came into the room with three cups of percolated coffee and a plate of chocolate biscuits on a silver tray.

"There's sugar and cream for anyone who wants some," she informed her visitors. "I'm making lunch for us and we'll eat in an hour or so. Hope that's suitable?"

"You're the boss," confirmed Randal, smiling for her benefit. He blew cheroot smoke into her face suggestively and she felt the heat in between her legs.

Stop it! Stop it or else I'll drag you to bed and tell them all to go, she squirmed to herself. Randal heard her thoughts and smiled even wider.

"Many thanks for your hospitality, Mrs Forbes. It's much appreciated," acknowledged Hadleigh.

"Call me Alison, and you're welcome."

"It's very good of you, Alison. Isn't it, Elvis?"

Elvis nodded, reluctant to speak after Randal's former rebuke.

Alison smiled and made her way back to the kitchen.

"OK then, Randal. I'll start with the obvious. What inspired you to write, especially as a child? Is it hereditary or just a natural flair?" asked Hadleigh, taking advantage of Randal's lighter mood and getting the ball rolling before his sarcasm and saturnine expression returned.

"No, 'the gift' is all mine," he replied with double meaning. "I always felt I should express myself on paper, even way back at primary school. Events and emotions just had to be put down that way. So rather than keeping a diary, I composed poetry."

"How old were you?"

"Six. But Mr Elvis Ford has already told you that previously, on my behalf."

"I'm just making sure. There's no room for error."

"Let's hope you don't make an error in this room," taunted Randal.

"I won't. I assure you of that. I'm confident I'll win you over."

"Are you now? Next."

"Did you have any specific influences? Other writers, say?"

"Just one. The author Paul Hargreaves. My agent's father. He pitched my work and the *Poetic Justice* series of poems were published. Others followed."

"At or after Oxford?"

"Both."

"Clive Hargreaves figures enormously in your life. Your relationship has stood the test of time, a rarity in this present day of fickle partnerships. What's he like as your agent and even more so as a friend?"

Randal's eyes threatened to spark, but he did not want to draw attention to his dislike of the question and arouse suspicion. "Clive's my loyal agent and closest friend. We understand and respect each other, ad infinitum."

"Oh, jumping ahead somewhat, how did you cope with his recent infirmity? You were present when he came out of his coma. That must have been mind-blowing."

"Quite."

"That's only a one-word reply, if you don't mind me saying."

"Quite."

"It's such a human-interest story. The reports on his miraculous awakening all differed. You were on the actual spot, so you can describe the event."

"If I wish to. And I don't. Next question," stewed Randal.

Hadleigh could see he had touched a raw nerve, so he moved on quickly. "How did you meet your wife? I'm only asking you this because she's instrumental, pardon the pun, in your joint legendary show *Priestess*. Her music with your lyrics. It's just spine-tingling."

"We met when I was a boy. I was ten and she was fifteen approximately. She was my mother's pupil. Mum taught private piano lessons from our front room at home. I used to listen to Alison a lot. I was besotted – schoolboy crush and all that kind of stuff. The relationship became serious when I was older and at Oxford. She was already famous and living in London. We got together and fell in love."

The interview continued in depth and Randal was disenchanted by the never-ending probing. Although Hadleigh was asking valid questions, it still felt like another form of intrusion. Elvis was clicking away from all angles, capturing Randal's smouldering image as he answered, but his patience was running ominously wafer-thin.

"Tell me, Randal, have any of your children inherited your gift for the written word?"

"I have," answered Roxanne, as she made her uninvited grand entrance into the conservatory. "I write little poems, just like my daddy. But I'm not showing them to you because you're the bad men who make my daddy mad, even though he's let you in! We both hate you! So, you can just go away now!" she glared.

This is the adopted daughter, so her poems are just coincidental and not hereditary. She's a feisty little thing, though, meditated Hadleigh.

Randal picked up on his thoughts and stubbed out his cheroot. He sprung up from his chair and approached Roxanne. He looked extremely angry. "You shouldn't be here! Now go and help Mummy with lunch!" urged Randal, feeling annoyed that she had made herself available for questioning in front of a prying journalist and a tedious photographer.

"But they are the bad men, Daddy." She frowned.

"No, they're not! Now do as I say! I know what I'm doing!" he snapped.

Roxanne's bottom lip jutted out. She was not used to his strictness, only his love. "I'm going then! I know when I'm not wanted," she sniffed, on the verge of tears.

Randal heard the clicking of the camera, as Elvis Ford took multiple photographs of her sad little face. He felt the rage rush through his body and turned round to confront the culprit. "Delete those images. *Now!*" he barked. "Absolutely no family photographs! That was an important precondition!"

His eyes kindled with intense light, knocking Elvis completely off-balance. He could not control his anger and Elvis felt a strange, alien force filter through his whole head. It was like a crackling, static surge, coupled with a high-pitched noise of unbearable intensity, flooding his brain and line of vision. He moaned as he clasped both hands around his head before he fell to the ground.

Roxanne smirked and forgot to cry. *Bad men should be punished!*

Hadleigh's jaw dropped open. He could have sworn that he saw Randal's eyes emit rays of bedevilled light and target Elvis.

"Oh God, he's having an epileptic fit! What should we do?" asked Hadleigh in a panic.

"We call 999, sit back and wait," replied Randal callously.

Hadleigh nodded and bent down towards Elvis's convulsing form. Roxanne stared at his camera. Then she focused in on Hadleigh's tape recorder. Her eyes glowed as she concentrated intently until they both exploded simultaneously into tiny pieces, totally decimating any film or recording.

Hadleigh covered his face instinctively to protect himself from the flying fragments and fell backwards, banging his head against the corner of a glass coffee table, causing him to pass out.

"Just look at this whole mess!" rebuked Randal. "You should *never* have interrupted my meeting! You know very well that if I'm talking to guests, then I've asked them here myself! I wouldn't have invited them in otherwise!"

Roxanne's bottom lip wobbled and she burst into floods of tears. She stormed up to him and stamped her foot down hard, then put her hands on her tiny hips. "I broke the camera and recorder for you! And now you're making me feel bad! I'm never going to help you again!" she yelled.

Hadleigh regained consciousness quickly, just in time to hear her words, and rubbed his head. *What the hell's going on here? How can a child destroy equipment by just staring at it with flashing eyes? At least that's what I thought I saw!*

Randal picked up on his quandary. He grabbed Roxanne by the arm and yanked her out of the room. "Stop crying! It's done. No more tantrums. You're making it worse because the man is suspicious. Don't talk about it anymore in front of him. OK?"

"Why are you so angry with me? I don't like it one little bit," she sobbed.

Randal relented and kneeled down to her height. "I didn't mean to shout at you, but you know I don't want any photographs taken of you, Ryan or Amber. Now I have to go back into the room and make this right. OK?"

"You're still angry with me," she pouted.

"I am, but I'll get over it. Now go to Mummy. I need to phone an ambulance."

"But you can make the bad man better."

"I can but that means using 'the gift'. He has to get better at the hospital."

"I suppose," she sniffed. "I'm going to Mummy; she doesn't shout at me like you."

Randal pulled her back and kissed her cheek, otherwise he would never hear the last of it.

"Is that better, Your Majesty?" he ribbed.

"A bit. I'm a good girl, really."

Randal half-smiled, then went back into the conservatory. Hadleigh had just about managed to ease himself into a chair.

"Are you OK?" asked Randal.

"I… erm… think so," he groaned, rubbing his head.

Elvis was still writhing on the floor, as Randal phoned for emergency care.

"I think this interview is pretty much null and void, don't you? It should never have taken place."

Hadleigh frowned deeply. He was still extremely unsettled by both Randal's and Roxanne's identical illuminated vision. Randal was simmering again.

More intrusion and suspicion! I may have to eliminate them! One by one!

4

Carlton Flint was at home with his ecstatic family. His wife, Francine, could not get enough of him or do enough for him. She had still not shrugged off his complete and almost supernatural recovery. What else could she think? He had been unconscious for months, with a very slim chance of waking up, let alone retrieving any of his senses.

She could not take her eyes off him, partly to check on his continuing rude health but also to remind herself how handsome he looked, regardless of his weight loss.

My beloved husband. Back where he belongs.

Their daughters, Maddie and Zoe, were both at school. Even they were afraid to leave their father for fear of him relapsing. They had all been living in a heart-stopping pressure cooker, not knowing what the next moment would bring, praying constantly for their father's recovery.

Then some kind of angelic intervention had occurred and brought him back to life!

For such a close family this was heaven on earth, but regardless of their tight connection, not one of them had ever realised the extent of Carlton's powers. He had always wanted it to be that way. All of his life he had kept his benefaction a closely guarded secret. He frowned deeply with his thoughts.

Except now I've been exposed to three very different outsiders. One who saved my life, and two others who are hellbent on snuffing it out!

Dr Winston Ramsey was an undisputed loyal ally. Carlton needed him to continue in his discreet corner and he was sure of his prudence. Randal Forbes was another barbaric ballgame, together with Roxanne, who worshipped him beyond the point of obsession. She knew no better, thanks to her paternal piece of work. The situation was a potential ticking time bomb of impending destruction.

Carlton was going to confide in Winston about his unsavoury rivals. He did not want to really involve him. Under less dangerous circumstances he would have kept him in the dark. But Winston was already asking questions about Randal's healing qualities, and Randal would be looking for answers with respect to Carlton's recovery.

Winston had witnessed Clive's remarkable restoration and was waiting patiently for Carlton to open up and put him in the complete, fascinating picture. And what a frightful eye-opener this revelation would be for the commendable consultant physician!

The more Carlton thought about bringing him in, the more he knew that ultimately it was the right thing to do. Randal would be boiling with assumption and conjecture as to the name of Carlton's saviour, who had provided the necessary assistance in order to help him reawaken.

He's incandescent with rage. I can feel his wrath reaching out through the telepathic airways. He won't rest until he knows how I did it or discovers the name of the person who helped me live. So, it's best that Winston should be prepared and that he knows exactly what we'll both be up against. A psychic killing machine with no conscience or respect for human life.

The telephone interrupted his thoughts. Fortuitously the caller was Winston.

"Hello there, Carlton! How are you today? Progressing nicely, I hope?"

"Good morning, Winston. I'm fine, just fine, back to normal. In fact, I was going to give you a call. When are you free? There are some very important issues I need to discuss with you. The sooner, the better."

"Oh?"

"It's about Randal Forbes."

"You sound stressed. Have you seen him? He's not upset you, has he?"

"Let's just say I've been on his wavelength since I came back to life."

"Are we talking telepathic mind games again?"

"Words to that effect."

"Now I'm very curious. I'm free this weekend. In fact, I'll be in your neck of the woods on Saturday. I'm lecturing at the hospital's postgraduate hall, late Friday afternoon, so I thought I'd book into a hotel overnight."

"Why don't you stay with us? Francine would love to see you again, and the girls will be more out than in, so we'll have lots of time to discuss things. Having you here with me, well, it's the very least I can do. My door will always be open to you. That's a lifelong promise. Please say 'yes'," urged Carlton.

"Well, how can I refuse an invitation like that? We do need to talk and I'll run a medical eye over my prize patient. Not that you'll need it. I'm confident of that."

"Excellent. I'll email you my full address and directions. I'm really looking forward to being with you again."

"Me, too. I'll see you on Friday about five. Oh, I have to go now. My registrar has just paged me. Thanks, Carlton, for your kind invitation and hospitality."

"Pleasure."

Carlton put down the phone and took a deep breath. How was he going to explain to Winston about Randal's darksome legacy? There was no point in holding back. Up until now, Randal's opposition had been nil. All his life he had ruled the infernal roost. Well, it was time for an untarnished change of authority, for an upright successor to turn the tyrannical tide.

Obviously, Winston would be unable to defend himself against such a mighty force, but forewarned would be forearmed. Anyway, Carlton had a good idea how to equip him with an adapted resistance to Randal's telepathic incursion.

Like it or not, we've both joined a long line of targeted, sacrificial victims. Two more potential subjects to add to Randal's monstrous catalogue of fatalities.

★★★

Ashley and Carlton both received a letter from Spencer's solicitors on exactly the same day. The covering note said it had been lodged with them for safekeeping: not to be opened, but forwarded to the named recipients, after Spencer's death. As he had tragically passed away, they had followed the wishes laid out in his will.

Enclosed for their attention was a personal letter from Spencer, together with a list of Randal's alleged sacrificial lambs. They had been named in the order they had died, along with the reason for their deaths. Ashley's hands trembled as he digested the paperwork before him.

Dear Mum & Dad,

You'll be reading this letter if I've succumbed to Randal's violation of another life. My own.

A copy of this correspondence will be posted to Carlton Flint in the hope that he's fully recovered, as he knows all this to be true. Please find attached a list of Randal's victims, minus my name. You can add that to it, if you finally believe me.

From a small boy to date, Randal has knowingly committed

the most abominable murders. He's acutely telepathic but uses his powers to invade his victims' heads with evil intent, and then he controls their thoughts by issuing commands. They are all sitting ducks, completely invaded, and will do exactly as he tells them to do, resulting in their deaths, or injurious harm.

His psychosis is significant, although he doesn't realise it. His blood daughter, Roxanne, has the same corrupt disposition, egged on and exacerbated by his dominance of her inheritance. He killed Maxine and Saul to claim her.

I worked closely alongside the late Detective Inspector Ronald Grey for five solid years, trying to prove Randal's guilt and validate all the homicidal activity. It was impossible because he was very rarely on the actual spot. As long as he had a photographic image, he could execute his plan of extermination from a safe distance.

Every single one of his targets who suspected his demonic leanings was assassinated or maimed.

Clive Hargreaves is his besotted lover and protector. He knows exactly what Randal has done but will never betray him. Alison doesn't have a clue about it all.

I'm sorry to write this letter, Dad, because I know how close you are to Randal's father, your dear brother Edward, but his son is a cold-blooded murderer and as long as he lives, more people will die. They will be ruthlessly eradicated in his twisted sense of poetic justice. If you read the poems in his books of the same name, focus in between the cryptic lines because it's all there.

Please don't let my death be in vain. Look into this for me and try to understand why I had to write it all down. It's horrendous but true.

When Carlton's able to talk, liaise with him and he'll verify my claims. I forgive you for not believing me. Randal's a convincing and compulsive liar. He's hoodwinked you all.

Your loving son, Spencer

Ashley's heart was thumping so hard in his chest he thought it would burst through his rib cage. He steeled himself to read the death list that Spencer had put together.

Jeremy Newton. Schoolboy bully at Tarnside Primary School. Mentally disturbed to date. Randal entered his brain and caused irreversible damage.

Alice Hardman. Headmistress of Tarnside Primary School. Deceased. She was completely naked when she jumped off the diving board into the swimming pool and drowned. She more than suspected his dark leanings, so Randal got rid of her. Verdict: suicide.

John Sterling. Dean's real father, a married man with three children. Deceased. Randal somehow caused his death by making sheets of exploding glass pierce his jugular vein. He had needed to protect his unmarried, pregnant Aunty Dottie. She had an affair with Sterling, who wanted no involvement with his baby and had offered her money to get a back-street abortion. Randal removed him, probably done through a photographic image to avenge his Aunty Dottie. Verdict: murder (unsolved).

Heather Marshall. Randal's maternal cousin. Disfigured for life. Bitten savagely by her two tame Labradors. They initially attacked Randal, so he reversed the process. I know it's hard to believe, but I feel he can enter any brain, human or animal.

Simon Holmes. Loutish pupil at Redwood Private School. Mentally disturbed to date. Randal probably punished him for something or other.

Raymond Haynes. Imprisoned for killing his wife. Verdict: murder.

Delia Haynes. Stabbed to death. Verdict: murder.

Nick Haynes (child). Drowned. Verdict: misadventure.

Jill Haynes (child). Drowned. Verdict: misadventure.

Lorraine Haynes (child). Drowned. Verdict: misadventure.

Randal was livid that Nick Haynes had overheard his

parents talking about Dean's real father, John Sterling. Nick subsequently gossiped about his murder at school. Dean was devastated because he knew nothing about it. Dottie had always hidden it from him. Dean has been Randal's lifelong mission, so he worked out a plan to annihilate the whole Haynes family. He caused Raymond Haynes to fatally stab his wife, Delia. Then some months later, he additionally hypnotised their three children to walk, unaided, into a lake and drown.

Robbie Sterling. (Dean's half-brother). Deceased. Quite by chance, Randal hooked up with him at Beaumont College, Oxford. When he realised the connection, especially as Robbie had shown an interest in Randal's sister, Patricia, he caused Robbie to jump off the edge of a cliff in the Lakeland Fells. He died instantly in the valley below. Verdict: accidental death.

Marcus Pennington, son of Lord and Lady Pennington. Institutionalised for murder and arson. Randal befriended him at Beaumont College. Marcus's grandfather was a priest and invited him to Clarendon Hall with the sole purpose of looking into his unholy aura. As a result, Randal entered Marcus's head, causing him to threaten his grandfather at loaded gunpoint, tie him to a chair and then set fire to the rectory after soaking it in kerosene. Then Marcus, still under instructions, hanged himself from a tree at the bottom of the garden but didn't die. Marcus has no memory of the night in question. I believe Randal has caused permanent amnesia by powerful hypnosis.

The Reverend Leslie Stainthorpe. Deceased. Murdered by his grandson Marcus Pennington. I believe, as did Inspector Ronald Grey, that Randal is in a long-term adulterous relationship with Marcus's mother, Lady Pennington, regardless of the age gap. She doesn't have a clue as to his evil exploits against her father and son. Randal has cruelly befriended Marcus again. Verdict: manslaughter with diminished responsibility.

Don Cannon. Deceased. Car bomb. Randal was involved because Don was making legal waves over Saul Curtis and claimed he was still contracted to himself. So, Randal wanted him out of the way permanently. Verdict: murder (unsolved).

Chief Inspector Leonard Galloway. Deceased. The first police officer to suspect Randal's dark side after the Haynes family murders, alerted to it all by Dr Patrick Shaw, who had grave doubts about Randal's disposition. He was killed in his car on a level crossing by a train, with Dr Shaw. The train driver said the car was just parked stationary. An accident waiting to happen. Verdict: misadventure.

Dr Patrick Shaw. Deceased. Killed alongside Leonard Galloway. Patrick was Victoria's (Randal's former nanny) husband. He felt that Randal had a dark side and was forever disagreeing with Victoria about its origin. Victoria thinks that Randal is special and uses his psychic abilities to help mankind. Patrick thought him to be evil and was living in great fear that he would discover his suspicion and delving. Patrick liaised with Leonard and they had compiled a substantial file of possible proof. I believe that Randal cultivated the whole episode on the level crossing by entering Patrick's head to effectuate the disaster and therefore all proof would die with them in the burning wreck of their car. I think the file was destroyed there and then.

Maxine Hale. Deceased. Randal caused her to jump off a suspended platform, on stage, in front of a huge audience. She broke her neck in the process by rolling down the steep staircase. I believe she slept with Randal and got pregnant with Roxanne as a result. She passed the baby off as her husband's, namely, Saul Curtis. Randal wanted full custody as Roxanne had inherited his dark powers. Also, he could not risk Maxine blabbing to Alison. Verdict: suicide.

Saul Curtis, Trevor Cannon and Detective Inspector Ronald Grey. All deceased and found at the cemetery where Maxine Hale is buried. I truly believe that Randal led the three of them there to eliminate them. I think he hypnotised the doomed trio, but I believe he could also have had help from

Roxanne, who wanted Saul out of the way so she could live permanently with her real father. As a result, Trevor Cannon could have killed Saul, believing he had car-bombed his father; Ronald Grey killed Cannon, and then shot himself through the head. Verdict: multiple murders (case unsolved).

That is the exact point when I became paranoid about what Randal was going to do to me. The family were all invited to his parents' for Christmas, one week after the murders. I was literally terrified of his presence and blanked out all my thoughts. I had a breakdown of sorts and hid myself away.

I noticed the striking resemblance between him and Roxanne – more than just physical features. She looked like the reincarnation of his satanic soul. That's what Inspector Grey believed too.

Miraculously, Carlton Flint came to see me and told me he had the same powers as Randal, and not to be afraid because he would help me. It was so healing to know that there was someone out there who believed me and had my welfare at heart.

Carlton Flint befriended me when I was terrified of Randal finding out that I'd been tracking his crimes. Carlton's gift is used for wholesome, righteous and wonderful acts of humanity. He's also hidden it, but for entirely different reasons.

On his last television broadcast, he was nearly fatally injured by a falling suspended monitor, which hit him on the back of his head and put him in a coma. I believe that either Randal, or Roxanne, caused the destabilisation of the mount and deliberately tried to murder him. I know that Carlton's aware of Randal's powers because he has the same gift, and he knew from the moment he met Randal that he was monstrous and demonic. I believe that Carlton has the power to heal himself and then he'll verify all my findings.

If I die before Carlton can talk, then Randal has got to me first. He'll stop at nothing to protect his hidden, lethal legacy. So, I'll be the next name on his psychic hit list. But not the last. Mark my words.

Ashley was horrified. He did not know what terrified him more: the possibility that Spencer had been completely insane or the horrific feasibility that Randal was everything Spencer believed him to be. Ashley was beside himself with agitation, alarm and grief. He had to see Carlton right away but also be very careful how to approach him. He had only just recovered from out of a comatose state and would need constant care with no added stress.

Ashley had no need to be concerned because upon reading Spencer's copy letter, Carlton picked up the phone and rang him first.

"Hello, is this Ashley Forbes? I'm Carlton Flint and a friend of your late son, Spencer. May I offer my deepest condolences to yourself and the whole family on your tragic loss. I have to talk to you about Spencer's letter. It's very important," explained Carlton earnestly.

Ashley thought he was going to pass out. He found his voice. "Is it about my nephew, Randal?"

"Yes. It is. We need to meet."

"Firstly, let me say how very glad I am that you're on the road to recovery, Mr Flint. I know how unwell you've been," replied Ashley on automatic pilot.

"Thank you so much. I'm much better. Now, about Spencer's letter. Mr Forbes, we urgently need to discuss it fully."

"Mr Flint, I need to know if my son's sanity was compromised," whispered Ashley.

"No! Your son was sane and brave. He stuck his neck out to defend my family over the suspended monitor disaster that put me in a deep coma, at the risk of Randal's wrath. Everything in his letter is the truth. Your nephew is a monster, a pitiless, relentless, telepathic assassin with no regard for anyone's life except his own, and certain individuals who he cherishes and loves in his own possessive and obsessive manner. His attractive persona, boundless charm and genius, hides a streak of pure, undiluted evil," stressed Carlton.

Ashley's heart stalled. It seemed to stop beating altogether. How could this horrendous description of his beloved nephew be true? Words deserted him and he could not reply. Carlton felt his appalling horror through the phone.

"Look, Mr Forbes, please meet with me. I know this is a terrible shock to your system, but I can explain to you, face to face, what we're up against here."

"We?" croaked Ashley.

"Yes, *we*, because once Randal knows that he's under suspicion, the red mist kicks in and he reverts to assassin mode."

"Oh, dear God. I'm devastated. How can any of this be true? How do you know for sure? How? Nothing has ever been proved in all these years!"

"Meet with me. Please! It's imperative that you do, and the sooner the better. What are you doing this afternoon? I don't live too far away from you."

"This afternoon? Wait... yes... I need to sort this out. I'm confused and traumatised and so very, very disturbed."

"Don't be, Mr Forbes. I'll help you. I'll explain things to you that I've only disclosed to one other human being. You have my full support and now write this down. I live at 16 Coral Grange, Didsbury."

Ashley took down the details then replaced the receiver with trembling hands. His whole body shook uncontrollably.

Dear Lord, what if Spencer and Carlton are right? Or are they both into mad conspiracy theories?

Carlton's an astrologer and I don't believe in horoscopes, or zodiacs, or any of those hippy-trippy, crazy ideas. It's all bloody rubbish. Absolute hogwash. Did Carlton egg Spencer on with unproven conjecture? I've got to know.

But that list! That sickening, homicidal series of names! All of them connected with Randal. Even I remember the names from several conversations over the years with Edward. But that doesn't mean that Randal actually murdered them! Does it?

Ashley brought a bottle of malt whisky out of his drink's cabinet. He poured himself a small glass and knocked it back in one go. He would be driving to Carlton's so he had to be vigilant, but he really felt like drinking the whole bottle.

He badly wanted to phone Edward, but where would he begin to explain all this conjecture? Edward would go ballistic and call him a traitor, and never speak to him again. His whole family would be decimated. This was a nightmare of the worse kind. But then he remembered that freakish gaze in Randal and Roxanne's eyes after Spencer's funeral. It was almost alien.

What had Spencer said to him about Randal's eyes? When he had asked Ashley, had he ever really noticed them? Ashley had replied that it was the Forbes colouring, so what was the big deal? Spencer had said, "Our eyes don't glow when we're annoyed." Ashley did not know what to believe, so he recited the Lord's Prayer for Randal to be absolved of all this conjecture.

Carlton told Francine to expect an immediate visit from Ashley Forbes. He had to be economical with the truth.

"He needs to talk to me about his son, Spencer."

"You mean Randal's cousin? The barrister who was taken off our court case? He jumped off a motorway bridge and committed suicide."

"I know, but his father feels bereft and guilty. Apparently, Spencer had good intentions with the case and wanted to do his very best for me."

"But he was going to represent Techscreen, and they have been found guilty of negligence." Francine frowned.

"I know that, so does Ashley, but he still wants to thank me for helping Spencer through his depression and for taking the time to understand his condition."

"You helped him? When? You didn't say."

"No, I didn't say because he was very disturbed and nobody would listen to him about his personal problems, so he confided in me alone. I guess that's why he lashed out at Astral TV after my injury. It was an impulsive, reciprocal gesture so that he could win a large amount of compensation to help you pay for my private medical care. He meant well even though he went about it all in the wrong way."

"I see."

"So, the least I can do is comfort his father and help him through his grief."

"As long as it doesn't tire you out. Remember, you've only just recovered. I feel for this man, but you come first. Also, Dr Ramsey will be here soon. Are you sure you won't be too exhausted with both visitors?"

"I won't be. I'll just be kind. Now, go and put the kettle on and make us both a cup of tea. Oh, with some of your homemade cherry cake. Please?" He smiled widely and she returned the gesture.

Carlton watched Francine as she made her way to the kitchen. He hated lying to her, but it was necessary. He looked at his watch. He had told Ashley to come at three o'clock – that way he would be able to talk to him privately for a while. By the time Winston arrived, Ashley would be fully aware of the Randal-effect.

Carlton had faxed a copy of Spencer's correspondence to Winston personally, so that he would also be in the full noxious picture. As a result, Winston had called him instantly to express his shock and disbelief at such a trail of unpunished atrocity. He was absolutely taken aback at the likelihood of such a chain of destruction.

If Winston had not been a witness to two supernatural recoveries, Carlton's in particular with their telepathic communication, then he would have dismissed Spencer's correspondence as the ramblings of a paranoid schizophrenic living with a severe personality disorder. Carlton was so positive of Randal's guilt and total involvement that Winston felt honour-bound to study all the facts very closely. His mind was now wide open to all paranormal possibilities.

Half an hour before Ashley's visit, Carlton felt Randal invade his head. He had been expecting contact but not at such an awkward and crucial time.

How goes it, starman? Welcome back to 'Planet Virtuous'. Did you enjoy your holy hibernation? Make the most of it. I'm in my metaphorical removal van and there's not a stick of furniture in sight. It's empty, awaiting your lifeless body.

Carlton responded. It was imperative that Randal did not pick up on suspicious intent. He had to communicate with him as quickly and effectively as possible.

I know who caused my 'accident'. I know it wasn't you. Roxanne got there first, didn't she? I bet you weren't expecting that one! Got one over on you, too, eh? Outdone by your own devil daughter.

She did it out of love for me but pure hatred for you. She meant well. Such a pity your head wasn't a few inches nearer the screen.

How do you sleep at night, Randal?

In a king-size bed with goose-feather pillows.

Your day of reckoning will come.

You reckon?

You've got away with far too much, for far too long.

And who's going to stop me? You? I'll see you in hell first. Wait… no… scrub that. You'll be one of those dozy, devout angels, sitting on a fluffy-white cloud, spreading love and light to the nauseating, upright masses.

I'm not going anywhere now that I've clawed my way back.

With a little help from a friend. Now, who would that be?

Nobody. The resurrection was all mine.

Liar! You needed another pair of hands to complete your healing process. I'll find out, starman, and when I do, I'll remove you both.

I'm here to stay. Get used to it.

I will. Temporarily.

I'm bored with this conversation now. Have I permission to close it down?

For the moment, starman. But I'll be back.

Good afternoon, Randal.

Fuck you, Carlton!

And you!

Randal withdrew from his brain and Carlton breathed a sigh of relief and release. The whole situation was dire and dangerous.

Francine walked into the room with tea and cake. "You look flushed, Carlton. Are you sure you're OK?"

"I'm fine, honestly. Just carry on doing your own thing. I'll sit here and wait for our guests."

"Oh… Ashley Forbes is here now. He's just getting out of his car. He looks like Randal but older. There's definitely a strong resemblance," observed Francine, peering through the window.

Carlton got up to see. Francine was right. It must be a Forbes family thing. He felt sick to the stomach at the likeness. But it was not Ashley's fault.

"I'll let him in," she said, and went to open the door.

Carlton walked over to receive his guest. Ashley looked deathly pale and his palm was sweating as they shook hands.

"I'm so glad you could come." Carlton spoke warmly. "I'm sorry that we've had to meet through such sad circumstances. Please sit down and make yourself comfortable."

Ashley looked a million miles away from at ease with the world.

"Would you like a cup of tea and some cake, Mr Forbes?" asked Francine.

"No. No, thank you. It's very kind of you, but I'm fine," replied Ashley, looking totally disconnected.

"Will you excuse me while I see to my baking? I'm not being rude, it's just that I have to keep an eye on it all," she explained, knowing they needed privacy so that Ashley could talk to Carlton openly.

"Of course. I understand," replied Ashley politely, when all the time his heart was skipping beats inside his chest wall.

Carlton picked up on his distress. *You poor, tortured soul, grieving for your treasured son and now considering the insane possibility of your much-loved nephew being his assassin, a mass murderer with no sense of right or wrong.*

Ashley spoke first. "Mr Flint, I need to know everything that Spencer spoke to you about. I desperately have to know the truth," he pleaded.

"First of all, call me Carlton. I insist. That's why I've asked you here today, Ashley. Is it OK to call you by your first name?"

"Yes. I prefer it. Carlton, please help me understand what's been going on here. I'm more than disturbed by all of this conjecture."

"I know you are. I can feel your distress. I also know that you doubt my theories, both my astrological background and, more so, my accusations against your nephew. But let me assure you that everything we discuss here today is confidential, and I'll answer any of your questions both truthfully and emphatically."

Ashley took a deep breath. "You've read Spencer's letter. Do you really think that Randal is evil? Do you honestly expect me to believe that he deliberately and callously killed my son? That he would bring me such grief and unbearable sorrow? That he would use a part of his brain, psychically, in order to bring about Spencer's suicide and the deaths of all those people on that hideous list? Do you absolutely maintain this to be true?"

"Yes! I do! Undoubtedly! Your son was not unbalanced. If he suffered any mental health issues, it was due to Randal's remorseless intimidation, not the irrational ideas of developing psychosis. Randal caused Spencer's unstoppable fear and ultimately affected his demise, to make it look like the inevitable suicide. He's relentless in his quest for other-worldly domination. He calls his demonic leanings 'the gift'. He'll protect his legacy at all costs. He thinks nothing of removing anyone who suspects, or wishes, to unearth his powers, to what he sees as an undeserving world."

Ashley shook his head disbelievingly. "I just can't get my brain around all of this. I've known Randal since he was a baby. We're a close family. He's always shown me respect and affection. My wife and I are so proud of him. We love him! His achievements are outstanding. His fame has never altered his attitude towards us all. If anything, it's made him even more magnanimous. With respect, Carlton, I know you're an expert in your own field of astrology, but I don't believe in such things. I think it's dangerous. How does it give you the right to predict circumstances or accuse people of such abominable crimes?"

"Astrology has nothing to do with this whatsoever. Look, Ashley, I'm taking a huge chance here today, but it's necessary. All my life I've had the gift of, shall we say, for the sake of argument, second sight? I'm not unique. There are others like me, Randal being one of them. I see my telepathic powers as a way of healing the world. Randal uses his to destroy and corrupt. I really don't know why he's adopted such an evil version of his benefaction. I truly think he's psychotic, with multiple personality disorders. Why else would he go out of his way to murder people who are simply curious about his gift? I know this must all sound crazy to you, but I've had numerous telepathic conversations with him, as well as face-to-face confrontation. He can't bear the fact that he's not the sole attraction, and even worse, in his mind, is the unpardonable sin that I use 'the gift' righteously."

"But these things just don't happen in real life! I mean, what proof can you actually give me that you're telepathic? How do I know that you're a healer? How?"

"I healed myself. I should have died, but I reversed the process and lived."

"But… but…"

"Ashley. I'm expecting another visitor soon. His name is Dr Winston Ramsey and he helped save my life. He'll answer some of your questions."

"I thought you said that you healed yourself?"

"I still had to have certain conventional help. Getting back to Dr Ramsey, he's a man of science – a down-to-earth, no-nonsense consultant physician – but he's experienced the unexplainable. I want you to meet him and discuss your doubts. We're both risking our reputations in order to help you believe."

Ashley's head was pounding. He had never felt such bewilderment or cluttered anarchy within his racing thoughts. A vision of Spencer flashed into his head, pleading with him to understand his fears about Randal. Now there was the letter with the death list. Was Spencer insane? Had Carlton lost his mind as well? What the hell was he dealing with here?

"Think of something that only you would know. Anything," requested Carlton, picking up on all of Ashley's doubts.

"Why?"

"Because I will hear and see it all telepathically."

"To prove you can read my mind?"

"To prove I can read your mind."

Ashley went along with his request. He badly needed some solid proof of all this speculation.

He thought of his childhood with his brothers, Edward and William. It was his eldest brother, Randal's father, who had always protected him from any harm. He remembered holding Edward's hand as they'd walked through the park, one glorious summer's day a long time ago. They had stood at the railings in front of the lake, feeding the ducks. He'd felt so happy and safe.

But that memory had become tarnished over time, because it was the same lake in which the three doomed Haynes children had drowned in the middle of the winter under its icy waters. And now, Spencer had named them in his list of Randal's victims, which only added to the evil blemish.

Carlton looked deeply into Ashley's slate-grey eyes before he spoke. "You're thinking of your brother, Edward, and when you were both little boys. You had a lovely day, feeding the ducks in the park. You loved being with him because he made everything good and secure. But now that memory is soiled because of the Haynes family tragedy. All three children drowned in that lake one icy winter's day. And I can tell you that your nephew Randal effected their demise. Beyond any shadow of a doubt."

Ashley gasped. He struggled to breathe. He spluttered and began to choke and shake uncontrollably.

Carlton rushed to his aid. "Don't panic, just breathe. You're OK, Ashley. It's just the shock. Let me help you."

Ashley felt Carlton's hands on his shoulders. The heat emanating from them was intense. He looked at his electric-blue eyes that seemed to radiate with light. Then Ashley's whole body and mind stopped racing, as he began to breathe normally.

"Oh, dear God! You can see inside my head! You *can* heal. You're all you claim to be! Spencer believed in you so much! You helped my son! You were his only consolation when it should have been me! Please, Carlton… please tell me that you could be wrong about Randal? That you may be mistaken and are picking up mixed messages," pleaded Ashley.

"I wish I was entirely wrong. I really do. But I'm not," he said softly with an earnest and compassionate expression.

Ashley put his head in his hands and wept. How could this be happening? How? Carlton was adamant, as Spencer had been. Spencer. His beloved son.

"I can't get my head around Randal. How would he be able to cause this… this evil, sickening chain of events? To look at him it seems impossible. He's so handsome with the most agreeable smile. I've seen people, especially women, fall for his irresistible charms. Over and over again."

"He enters their heads via a photographic image. I've done it myself but to instil confidence into a desperate person who struggles to cope. In Randal's case it's usually to obey his commands, which inevitably leads to their demise. You've read Spencer's list, and how Randal achieved his barbaric aims. Do you think that list was just produced recently? While Spencer was disturbed? He'd been compiling it for five years, with the help of the late Detective Inspector Ronald Grey, and Chief Inspector Leonard Galloway before him. Randal removed them all. Those names are not the ramblings of your son's unsettled mind. They're the victims of your nephew's paranormal crimes, of Randal's vivid imagination, devising all different methods of extermination. He's a prize-winning demonic scriptwriter, setting out each scene, filling in the dialogue and creating the murderous conclusion. A flawed, dispassionate genius, hellbent on removing any potential threat or suspect, without compunction or guilt. He gets a manic, psychotic buzz out of the end result and subsequent fallout of his destructive projects of annihilation. It's his life's blood. He's a killing junkie, a vampire by proxy, bleeding his victims dry. He can't help himself. He doesn't wish to reform. I've tried and now I've had it with him, his constant threats and sardonic repartee," explained Carlton passionately.

The tears cascaded down Ashley's cheeks as the monstrous truth was beginning to dawn on him. *Randal! Edward's beloved son!* A demon who had fooled them all. Who had ended Spencer's life casually and callously without the slightest sense of criminality! Randal, who had attended Spencer's funeral with a feigned, artificial expression of anguish and sorrow, when underneath he was patting himself on the back for a job well done! Ashley felt as if his heart would break in two. It was unbearable. Unthinkable. Unutterable.

"I'm so deeply sorry, Ashley. I feel your pain," said Carlton with sincere sympathy.

Ashley pulled a handkerchief out of his pocket to dry his eyes. He blew his nose. "What about Roxanne? Is she really his daughter?" he croaked.

"Yes. She has the same powers. He's coaching her to abuse them."

"How?" But before Carlton could answer, Winston Ramsey

rang on the door. *We're all doomed. Three more names on a death list.* Ashley shuddered.

"That will be Dr Ramsey now. Francine will let him in," said Carlton.

Ashley felt he was living in a parallel universe and that everything around him was another version of his normal, orderly life except this existence was chaotic, murky and hideous. How was he going to hide all this from his family?

"How? How does he teach Roxanne? How can he coerce a child to perform such barbarous acts?" Ashley whimpered.

"She's inherited his psychosis along with her powerful legacy. She caused my so-called accident, in her eternal quest to impress her father," explained Carlton.

"How?" repeated Ashley robotically.

"By watching the last programme of *Celestial Bodies* on her television and staring intently at the screen. She destabilised the mount that held the large monitor into place. The astrological, cosmic-wheel diagram was displayed inside it. It sounds impossible. I know that, but this is her speciality. Moving objects with her mind. She wanted to kill me. They both still do."

Ashley's mouth fell wide open and he gasped before he found his voice. "You mean to tell me that Alison has no idea of his infidelity? Of his affair with Maxine Hale? Of the fact that she's adopted Randal's blood child under the pretext of compassion? They've been together for years! How could she possibly have no inkling as to his adultery? His bisexuality? His telepathic powers, or, for that matter, his sordid, deadly, monstrous butchery? How could she be so oblivious to all that?"

"You were, Ashley. You've known him far longer than Alison has," Carlton gently reminded him.

Carlton looked up as Francine showed Winston into the room, only to see Ashley hiding his face in both hands. His shoulders were convulsing and his sobs quite audible. Carlton waved her away.

"It's OK," he mouthed.

Francine looked at Winston, who nodded at her reassuringly.

"He's grieving. We'll help him through this. Don't worry," soothed Winston.

You poor man, losing a son, the worst thing in the world, and in such tragic circumstances, thought Francine, as she left them alone and closed the door.

Carlton kneeled down in front of Ashley and spoke to him with deep compassion. "Ashley. I know this is so very, very hard and cruel. Believe me, Spencer's tragic death will not be in vain. He was tortured and suffered a fatal ending in the name of his own quest for justice. Justice for all the victims in Randal's never-ending murderous story. It's of very little comfort to you and your family, especially along with the shock discovery of Randal's counterfeit affection."

"Does he actually care about anybody?" wept Ashley.

"He has a strange fondness and loyalty towards the people who have succumbed to his benevolent side. He does have a rare soft spot for you. He also has a strong sexual passion for his obsessive needs, and a Randal-version of love for Alison, his children, mostly for Roxanne and not forgetting Clive Hargreaves. But mark my words, when he's in homicidal mode, anybody could be eliminated should they dare to question or confront him on the origin of his unearthly powers. Spencer has brought the three of us together, to work out a way of resisting or even halting this dark escalation."

Ashley looked up slowly. His face was racked in pain. "Resisting him? Halting him? How? We're powerless! We're all walking targets! I can't believe I'm saying this to you! I can't believe that I believe you! But I do. I've been blind. So very, very blind. Why didn't I believe my beloved son?"

"I'm going to help you overcome his telepathic invasion. Both of you. Winston, you didn't hear my full conversation with Ashley. Everything in Spencer's letter and list is true. It's one hundred per cent accurate, and for all we know, there could be even more homicidal activity that has not been logged. It's my job now to stop any deadly intentions towards you both."

"How?" asked Ashley and Winston simultaneously.

"I've a recording of Randal when he was interviewed. I'll hypnotise you to ignore his voice, to literally dismiss it, if he enters your minds telepathically. You'll automatically disregard any instructions he wants you to perform. Your brain will cut off, rendering his commands hopelessly ineffective."

"But what about you, Carlton? Can you hypnotise yourself?" groaned Ashley.

"And what if he employs Roxanne to strengthen the effect?" added Winston.

"I have my own powers of defence. They're as vigorous as his. As for Roxanne, well, he's already tried to hurt me with her help. She wasn't strong enough. I caused her to fly across the room with my retaliation. She banged the back of her head really hard against the wall. I felt guilty for days afterwards. He'll not risk that circumstance again."

"Now I understand it all. That's why she made the screen fall on your head: to pay you back for her own injury," realised Winston.

"But she could still use her powers against us," whispered Ashley, looking at Winston through haunted eyes.

"Yes, she could. I will include that possibility in your hypnosis and instruct you to also ignore the voice of a little girl. Namely hers," Carlton reassured them.

Carlton asked them to sit together on the settee. He played Randal's recording and carried out a dual hypnosis.

It was simple, but he knew their protection was active and their telepathic response to Randal's commands would be duly compromised. And that was the best he could do for now. Apart from pray.

Then suddenly, Carlton had a change of plan. He clicked his fingers to bring only Winston out of his hypnotic trance.

"Is it done?"

"Yes, Winston. You're protected, but there's something I need to discuss with you. I've decided to wipe all of Ashley's memory banks clean. He's grieving so much for his son, and the discovery of Randal's culpability is killing him. It will affect his whole existence and compound his heartbreak. He's brought Spencer's letter with him. He won't remember. I'm going to destroy it. What possible good will it do? It won't alter anything and I'd rather he believed that Spencer was mentally unstable."

"But that means Randal's got away with his son's murder, while Ashley still carries on believing in his nephew's benevolence! He'll keep that sense of love and pride for him brimming over! How unjust is that?"

"It's not unjust. It's charitable. The man is bereft. His soul is irreparable. Why add more anguish to his frightful plight? I can't sit back and let him suffer, even with my protection. It's inhuman – in some ways more brutal than the truth. But I have to ask you, Winston, do you want me to do the same for you? That way, Randal will mean nothing and all suspicion of him will disappear."

"No. I need to be aware. Your protection is sufficient. I've seen the extent of your powers, and I'm in awe and want to learn more. I trust you, and feel safe. Randal's not my family, so I'm not devastated by his monumental treachery. I want him to get what's coming to him."

Carlton opened a drawer in his sideboard and brought out a camera. He took a full-face picture of Ashley.

"I'll enter his brain. He'll drive home safely, but the minute he switches off his engine, I'll effectively airbrush this whole despicable scenario out of his mind for good. That way he'll be saved from Randal's suspicion and wrath. He'll think he's just had a short drive round the block to get a newspaper, but they'd sold out."

Carlton snapped Ashley out of his dreamlike state. The look of torture returned but Carlton knew it would only be temporary.

"I'll keep in touch with you, Ashley," assured Carlton. "I'll help you get through this."

"I'm completely heartbroken and truly don't know which way to turn."

"I'll find a way to bring your nephew to justice. You don't need to tell anyone for now. Rest assured, the truth will prevail. I promise you that."

Ashley nodded and then said goodbye. He got into his car on automatic pilot and drove under a dark, lightless cloud of grief, devastated by Randal's evil deception.

He pulled up outside his house and for the moment was dazed. Then he looked perfectly normal but irritated.

Bloody newsagent! Fancy not having my favourite paper. I needn't have bothered coming out.

He walked up the path and put his key in the lock. Randal opened the front door at the same time, smiling at him. "Surprise! I just thought I'd come down and visit my fave uncle," he said warmly. "I was looking out the window and saw you walking up the path."

"Randal! How wonderful to see you! What a treat! Is Alison with you?"

"No, just me."

They hugged each other and Randal felt his uncle's deep grief.

"Uncle Ash, I'm so, so sorry about Spencer. I had to come and comfort you again. I know we weren't close, but I wish he was still with us all. I would do anything to spare you this pain. If you want to talk or ask my advice, I'm here for you. And that includes Aunty Julia and James."

Ashley bit his lip. "I do need your help, Randal. You have such a keen perception on life. Spencer actually made a will. A bloody will, would you believe? He must have been so disturbed to have had one drawn up at such a young age. Oh, dear God. Your Aunty Julia and I have failed him terribly. What did we do wrong? Where did we go wrong? Why has this happened?"

Randal put his arm around his uncle's shoulder. He hated to see Ashley suffer and genuinely wanted to comfort him.

"If anyone can make us all smile again, Randal, then it's you," croaked Ashley, as the tears cascaded down his cheeks. "I really don't know why Spencer couldn't get on with you. You're such a blessing in this family."

Randal hugged him even tighter and scanned his brain.

He suspects nothing. I'm so relieved. Now he can live. My dear Uncle Ashley.

5

Randal called at Clive's office to catch up with some appointments. He had been there only five minutes when Edward contacted him. Clive watched Randal intently on the phone. He was soft-soaping his father, who was very angry about the method of Spencer's departure.

"I know it's tragic," acknowledged Edward, "but he's left such a huge hole in your Uncle Ashley's life, and your Aunty Julia is inconsolable. We've tried our best to understand the gravity of Spencer's illness, but what son behaves in such a manner and breaks his parent's hearts into tiny pieces? And the way he treated *you*! Going all out to discredit and blacken your name! And you still found the time and compassion to visit your uncle and aunt to console them! It's so commendable, son."

"Dad, Spencer was sick. I mean, mentally and emotionally unbalanced. I don't think even he was aware of what he was going to do. You mustn't blame him for his seemingly selfish act. Pity him. Don't condemn him," replied Randal with a hidden smirk.

"You're such a good son, Randal. I know you didn't see eye-to-eye with your cousin. We all witnessed the antipathy between you both over the years, and yet you're still defending his last cowardly act. You're quite remarkable in every way, and don't let that go to your head. We love you just the way you are," responded Edward with a slight break in his voice.

"Dad, please be there for Uncle Ashley and Aunty Julia. Remember, they have James to console as well. He's lost his big brother and is now an only child, and even more precious to them both. They need your compassion, not your criticism. Spencer wasn't a coward; he was greatly disturbed. Bear that in mind. Always."

"Yes, son. You're very wise. I have to go now, but give our love to Alison and the children, and we hope to see you all soon."

"You will. Love you, Dad."

"Love you too."

Randal put the phone down and looked over at Clive, who was staring at him as though his eyes were glued open.

"What?" quizzed Randal.

"You know what!"

"I don't know what."

"I've had time to think about it all. It was you! It was you who made him jump! Spencer wasn't unbalanced. You ordered him to jump, just like Alice Hardman, Robbie Sterling and Maxine Hale. At least they avoided a line of rush-hour traffic. As jumping goes, that was a prize-winning performance!" berated Clive, his cheeks flushed with anger and his stress levels rising rapidly."

Randal felt his agitation and high anxiety, so he had to instantly placate him. "Clive, I had nothing to do with Spencer's motorway caper. He really was out of his skull. Any voices he heard in his hysterical head were not mine. They were all his own," lied Randal.

"I don't believe you."

"Fine. Then don't blame me for feeling unwell. This time you'll have to heal yourself."

"Swear to me. Swear you didn't do it."

"I swear."

"Swear like you really mean it."

"Fuck off! There! I've sworn like I really mean it!"

"Don't joke! Spencer's dead! He hated you and you loathed him, but he was still family. I'm your protector, so you owe me the truth. Don't try and tone it down!"

"I've told you the truth. If you choose to disbelieve me, it's your suspicious mind."

"Why did you cancel last week's morning TV appearance to suddenly go and drive down to see your Uncle Ashley? Was it your guilty conscience or were you making sure that he didn't actually believe Spencer's revelations?"

"My Uncle Ashley's suffering, and he's more important than talking crap on a televised sofa with a wannabe airhead. Look, Clive, just drop it! I've done nothing wrong, so I've nothing to defend!" he stressed with glittering eyes.

Clive took the threatening hint. *I have to believe him. I just have to.*

"Yes, Clive. You have to believe me," Randal answered his thoughts. "I hear your scepticism and I don't blame you for doubting me but I've no reason to lie to you. You know the whole score, the list of meddlesome interlopers who got what they deserved. But Spencer? Well, he's not one of them."

Clive nodded. His breathing became more regulated and his features less strained. "Some protector I am," Clive admitted. "I'm a disbelieving, screwed-up custodian."

"Stop right there! You're the guardian of 'the gift'. You're the best. I don't want you to relapse and it's not only your protective role I need. You know that. Don't you? Don't you, Clive?" said Randal softly, moving nearer.

Clive saw the tenderness in Randal's gaze. How could those misty, loving eyes cause so much destruction when they looked like this? He felt he was drowning in two pools of desire.

"I believe you," answered Clive hoarsely. "Spencer was his own enemy."

"Exactly. Spencer was his own enemy," whispered Randal, moving even closer, embracing his devoted defender before he took full possession once more.

★★★

Hadleigh Masterson could not get his head round the disastrous and mystifying interview with Randal. He knew beforehand that it would not be plain sailing, and his subject could be difficult: prickly with a caustic wit.

But he was far from prepared for the radiant emanation of light shafts that appeared to flood out of both Randal's and Roxanne's line of vision when they were both very displeased.

Mind you, I did blackout for a few minutes, but I'm sure, before I banged my head on the coffee table, that I saw Randal look at Elvis with luminous daggers, and that set off his epileptic fit. Then, Roxanne, with the same visual emphasis, seemed to decimate his camera and my tape recorder into a thousand pieces! How the hell did that happen?

He had picked up the phone several times to send his apologies, via Clive, to Randal, over the impulsive photographs Elvis had taken of Roxanne. He was out of order, but the reaction to it was very alarming. It was more than just an angry response. It was positively demonic.

Elvis was still in a bad way in hospital. Nothing seemed to be helping him recover. All treatment and medication were hopelessly ineffective. It was weird. In fact, it was eerie, strange and unearthly. Even the doctors could not understand his stupor and lack of response. His family were in touch constantly, asking Hadleigh questions which he could not answer properly.

What can I say, apart from that Elvis just collapsed?

Hadleigh's assistant knocked on his door and interrupted his contemplation. "Mrs Ford is asking to see you."

97

"Where is she?"

"In reception."

"You better send her in, then," sighed Hadleigh, but before she was invited, she barged into the room.

"Are you the editor of this rag? I need answers!" she snapped.

"Mrs Ford, please sit down," urged Hadleigh.

"Never mind all that! What happened to my husband's camera? Why was it smashed up?" she probed, pulling herself up to her diminutive five foot two inches.

"I don't know. It's all a blur. I slipped, banged my head and then I fainted."

"Slipped on what?"

"I don't know."

"You don't know! My husband's in a terrible state from just taking photographs of Randal Forbes and his camera is destroyed? You say you slipped on something? Is there a bloody ice rink in the middle of the room?"

"I know how it must seem." Hadleigh frowned.

"Oh, do you? Well, it seems to me that there's been some foul play here. It's all very unsatisfactory and I need to speak to Mr Randal Forbes. Now!"

"He's very hard to pin down, Mrs Ford."

"Oh, is he? We'll see about that!" she fumed.

"Mrs Ford, I mean, Gemma, leave it all to me. I'll get to the bottom of it for you, so please don't upset yourself any further. The hospital's doing everything they can for your husband. Let me sort it out. Please!"

"Well, you better had 'sort it out', Mr Masterton. You're the editor of *The Announcer* and it won't look good at all for your newspaper if I report this incident to another publication. Mark my words, that's what I'll do if I don't get the right answers!" she threatened, her eyes jet-black with anger.

"Gemma, this isn't going to help your husband improve. There'll be journalists swarming around us both if you take this action. Surely you wouldn't want that kind of constant intrusion?" replied Hadleigh, clutching at straws.

"I want whatever it takes to get to the bottom of this shameful puzzle."

"Firstly, let's see if Elvis gets better. I'm sure the doctors will bring him round. Then we can talk to him and he can throw more light on the event. Like I told you before, I was spark out, so I can't really explain what happened. He'll probably know more than me. At least give him a chance to rally round before you take drastic measures."

"What you mean, Mr Masterson, is for me to keep your precious paper out of the sordid limelight. Do you think I was born yesterday? How would you feel if it was your fiancée lying there in that hospital? Would you be so reasonable? Have you visited Elvis since? I can't look at him. It's as if his features have been replaced. He looks tortured and deranged. Who, or what, could do that to an optimistic man with a sunny disposition?"

"I don't know, but we'll find out for sure."

"How? How will you find out for sure? Only Randal Forbes knows the truth."

"Then we'll have to arrange a meeting with him to discuss this in depth."

"That's the best idea you've had yet. But I'm still reporting this to the police and my solicitor!"

"Leave it with me."

Hadleigh groaned inwardly. What had started out to be such a promising, unique interview with his idol, had turned into a nightmare situation. He had unwittingly put himself in the eye of a legal storm. His photographer was badly injured, but not from any physical intervention. How? Randal had not laid a finger on him.

Roxanne had not even touched the camera or tape recorder, yet they were both blown to smithereens.

If Elvis remained disabled and enfeebled, his wife would sue for damages. But from who? Who would she see as culpable? Would it be *The Announcer* for employing him or Randal for injuring him in some weird way? Or both?

And what exactly could I offer in my own defence? I'd have to say I was out stone cold, that I didn't see anything, even though I did. But what I thought I saw would be laughed out of court, so it's best that I play dumb. Gemma Ford's on the warpath looking for answers and she's one very determined battleaxe.

His fascination for Randal was rapidly evaporating. Something was freakishly amiss. He had admired him for many years, but was that veneration misplaced? Only time would tell.

★★★

Randal was in the Albert Hospital foyer, walking up and down on the spot. He was seething at himself for allowing Hadleigh Masterson to interview him, and the subsequent fiasco surrounding his photographer's infirmity.

Is there only one harrowing hospital in this city? Firstly Clive! Then the starman! And now 'snappy-happy-at-Graceland' Elvis Ford! All three of them in the same antiseptic building! Ridiculous! Utterly bizarre!

Randal contemplated on the outlandish situation. How to deal with an intrusive exclusive? His sense of theatre spurred him on, and the need to eliminate each problem fired him into action.

He visited the Albert Hospital disguised as a much older man, sporting a cloth cap over a salt and pepper full hairpiece that hid his vibrant red locks. A false moustache and glasses completed the masquerade, together with a set of clothes fit for a charity-shop sale.

He needed to know the names of all the physicians who had

been looking after Carlton when he was comatose, because he felt that one of them was his actual redeemer. If this associate was a medical man, as Randal suspected him to be, then he would be totally aware of Carlton's vigorous healing powers and had been a witness to 'the gift'.

The bile rose up in the back of his throat at the thought of his rival possessing the same supremacy. That alone was dire, without the added complication of an unwanted spectator and helper.

Randal walked into the reception area and saw the same woman behind the glass cubical who nearly lost her teeth when he was desperate to know the way to the intensive care unit, so that he could resuscitate Clive. She had been more interested in Randal's seductive attraction and celebrity, rather than pointing him in the right direction on that particular day.

This time he approached her and asked the way to the gents' toilets. She ignored him so he repeated his request curtly. She looked up slowly, noted his dishevelled appearance and scowled at him.

"I'm busy!" she said tersely. "Can't you read the signs yourself? I'm not here as a tour guide."

Randal just nodded and walked away. He was torn between elation that he was unrecognisable and the strong compulsion to decimate her empty head.

He sat down on the front row of seats in the waiting area and studied the names of the various consultants on duty. He was just about to get a coffee from the machine when in walked Dr Winston Ramsey with his registrar. They stopped and stood together, in deep, quiet conversation.

Randal recognised Winston as the medic who had examined him after his life-saving intervention for Clive. Randal looked away, but he was still listening intently to their words with his supersonic hearing.

"I think we'll try some physiotherapy today, and if it doesn't

101

work, we'll get him admitted into a psychiatric hospital. I'm not usually keen on that, but nothing appears to be functioning. I'm going up to the ward now and I'll have a word with his wife about it all. She's incensed and wants answers, so I'll have to tread very carefully," explained Winston.

"What exactly happened to him?" asked his younger colleague.

Winston lowered his voice, but Randal's psychic antennae could hear every single word.

"Well, he's a freelance photographer who was apparently on an assignment for the *Daily Announcer*. The editor is Hadleigh Masterson and they were interviewing Randal Forbes. At his home, no less."

"Randal Forbes! That was a scoop!"

"Hmm. Well, Mr Ford just collapsed and was stretchered in. He's in a pretty bad state, but personally I think the root cause is more mental than physical. He's been traumatised," confirmed Winston, sensing that Randal was behind the infirmity.

"Didn't Randal Forbes's agent, Clive Hargreaves, make that mind-blowing recovery not so long ago? Then, Carlton Flint, in the same bed, no less, blew that former miraculous convalescence out of the water! It must have been the most incredible moment for you when Flint woke up."

"More incredible than you'll ever know," responded Winston, with double meaning. "We kept it all away from the press, at Carlton's request. He didn't want the limelight. All he wanted was to get back to normality."

Randal took a sharp intake of breath. This vital discovery was staring him in the face. In fact, he had literally collided with the truth.

Dr Winston Ramsey! Carlton's medical man of the month! His altruistic ally! The legend of the Lancet! *Concealing the mystical moment from all the inquisitors!*

And now, Elvis Ford is also taking up a bed here in this holistic

*hellhole. And his witch of a wife is on the unworthy warpath. Gotcha!
Now, I'm gonna getcha!*

Randal clenched his fists with indignation. Blast them all
with a first-class, one-way ticket to Hades.

*I removed the Spencer threat, but now four more names have moved
into the fucking firing line. Carlton Flint, Winston Ramsey, Hadleigh
Masterson and the very undesirable Mrs Elvis Ford.*

*I was searching primarily for clues to Carlton's saviour, and I've
found him. But I've unearthed yet more prying eyes in the process. I need
a colossal thinking cap.*

He walked past Winston and deliberately bumped into
his shoulder. He carried on striding away from him. Winston
tutted but made no connection.

*I'll get you tutting alright! I'll teach you not to interfere in inequitable
business, you meddling, menial model of imperfection! You haven't a
clue what you're up against! I'll put you in your submissive place, Dr
Winston Ramsey! Flint's secretive sidekick! But firstly, I need to see
where Elvis Ford is, in this medical maze of misery!*

Randal bought a newspaper at the kiosk and then
purposefully waited for Winston to finish talking. He followed
him and watched as he entered the ward. He stayed outside,
leaning against the wall pretending to read. He was well-placed
to hear the discussion with the ward sister.

"I'm really glad you're here, Dr Ramsey. Mrs Ford's asking
a lot of questions again. Quite frankly she's unbearable, and her
manner isn't helping matters."

"We're going to move Mr Ford to a psychiatric hospital
shortly. We've examined him extensively and there's nothing
physically amiss. I'm satisfied that we've done everything we
can at our end. His problem's post-traumatic stress and it needs
thorough investigation. We're not able to supply that care, so a
transfer is definitely the next step."

"Oh, it's a psychiatric hospital now, is it?" interrupted
Gemma Ford, as she barged uninvited into the sister's room

through the open door. "Over my dead body!"

"Mrs Ford, all your husband's tests came back normal. The only thing that's grossly irregular is his mental health," explained Winston.

"And whose fault's that? I'll tell you who! It's that shithead Randal Forbes! Something very ugly happened in his house, and that stuck-up editor refuses to tell me what! But from his shifty expression, I know he's lying through his implanted teeth!"

"I'm afraid you'll have to take that up with him."

"If you transfer him to a funny farm, Dr Ramsey, I'll drag you through the front page of the tabloids. You're all the same! Positions of power, walking over the little man!"

"Mrs Ford. I think you should look at who the real culprit is here. It's not this hospital. We've done our best. If you're going to go down the blame-culture route, then I would suggest that you speak to Randal Forbes personally, and, if the editor is hiding something, then it could be that he also feels intimidated. He's dealing with a very powerful force of nature. Randal Forbes is a commanding personality, so be prepared for a legal battle."

"I'm not scared of him! He won't browbeat me! I've been to the police! Let them deal with the untouchable Mr Forbes!"

"Do what you think is best. Now, if you'll excuse me, I've paperwork to finish, including your husband's transfer to another hospital."

She flounced out muttering obscenities and passed Randal in the corridor.

Stupid banshee bitch! This will be easy. You need to be full-stopped.

He stared at the back of her head and began to rape her senses. His eyes flared with heated light, blinding disabling rays of intense radiance. She stopped walking and put both her hands around her ears and screamed. She fell to the floor and began writhing around on the spot in a perpetual circle of agony.

"Who's screeching?" puzzled Winston, but he was already making his way to the source.

Randal was still there, hiding behind his newspaper, practically scorching two holes through the pages. He stepped up on his assault, refusing to stop until he had reached the point of no return. Winston saw a crowd around a woman who was fitting on the carpet. He realised who she was and kneeled down to help her.

She lashed out at him with her fist, caught him under his chin and then smacked him in his right eye. It was impossible to subdue her. Then she stopped breathing altogether. Her head rolled to the side and her eyes stared at him, but they saw nothing.

He tried to revive her, but he knew she had gone. Randal slipped away unnoticed. His visit had been twofold fruitful. He had come to find out the name of Carlton's ally, only to eliminate yet another unexpected, menacing threat.

Spencer's prosecuting at the pearly gates. Mrs Ford has deservedly joined him in the queue. Mr Ford and his camera won't ever recover. Three down and three to go. Only Flint, Ramsey and Masterson left. That virtuous trio. Soon to be a double act. Followed by a solo one. Oh, shucks. And then there were none!

★★★

Roxanne needed to talk to Randal. For the last few days, she had seen the same girl walking near her new school, looking drenched and dishevelled. Then today, as she looked through the classroom window, she saw the girl again pressed up against the railings. She clearly heard her voice, crying for help. Roxanne put her arm up to speak to her teacher.

"Excuse me, Miss Ragdale, there's a girl outside crying. She looks really upset and her clothes and hair are wet."

The teacher walked over to the window and looked in

the direction Roxanne had indicated, but there was nobody present.

"I can't see her, Roxanne. Where exactly do you mean?"

"Over there! She's crying and shaking the railings, and I've seen her before."

Miss Ragdale followed her gaze but saw nothing. "Roxanne. I can't see anyone. Maybe you've made her up? You're such a clever girl with a wonderful imagination. Perhaps she's an invisible friend and you're the only person who sees her? Now there's no harm in that, but not when it stops our lesson, so be a good girl and sit back down."

Roxanne frowned deeply. If Miss Ragdale could not see the girl, then what was she seeing? Was she real?

But I can still see her. She's there and she's crying. And she's wet. Really wet.

★★★

That same evening at home, Roxanne asked Randal's advice.

"Daddy, I think I've seen a ghost."

Randal looked up from his book. She had his full attention. "A ghost?"

"Do you believe in them?" she puzzled.

"It depends. I don't use the word ghost. They're just… lost."

"Lost?"

"Yes. They want to move on but perhaps are stuck between here and where they should be."

"You mean like a train that's broken down and makes you late?"

"Well, not quite a train. They're on a journey but not as we know it."

"Where to?"

"From here to eternity."

"Where's that? Is it near Weybridge?"

106

Randal laughed out loud. Sometimes she really cracked him up, usually when she did not realise how funny she was being.

"It's not a joke. This girl is really, really upset," she admonished him.

He stopped laughing and tried to look more serious for her sake. "Where have you seen her exactly?"

"Outside my classroom window, at the railings. She was shaking them and then walked up and down."

"What makes you think she's a ghost?"

"Because I showed her to my teacher, but she couldn't see her. But she was there!"

"I believe you, pumpkin."

"What should I do? She needs help. I know she does."

"Do you want me to look for her with you?"

"Can we go tomorrow?"

"Tomorrow's Saturday, and the school will be closed."

"But she doesn't know that. She might still be there."

Randal nodded. She was right. Spirits did not have timetables. "OK then, we'll go tomorrow. How's that?"

"Oh, thank you, Daddy. You'll see her. Other people just don't."

The next day Randal drove to the school. The weekend traffic was heavy, but Roxanne did not care. It was just her and Randal in the car. She had him all to herself.

She put her head on his shoulder and he kissed the top of it. This was her idea of heaven. No interruptions. Nobody pulling him away. No endless telephone calls. No diversions. No intrusion. Just the two of them. She loved him deeply, and just when she thought she could not love him anymore, her adoration would go up another notch. And today they were ghost hunting. Would any other father and daughter be doing that? She didn't think so.

Randal switched up the car radio, wound down the window and lit up a cheroot.

"You don't mind me smoking, do you, pumpkin?"

"No, Daddy. The smoke reminds me of you, so I love the smell."

He smiled his special smile and her heart sang as she moved even closer to him. *He's Ryan's and Amber's daddy too. But today he's all mine!*

They reached their destination and Randal parked the car. Roxanne showed him the place where she had seen the girl, but she was not there.

"She was here! Right here! I promise!"

Randal felt the hairs on the back of his neck stand to attention. The feeling persisted and Roxanne picked up on his psychic vibration.

"What is it, Daddy? Can you see her?"

"Shh... quiet. I can hear her."

Roxanne slipped her hand into his. She looked up at him as he spoke.

"Her name's Mistral Sommers," he whispered. *I remember that name. Why?*

"Mistral Sommers," repeated Roxanne. "Why can't I hear her?"

"She's lost and she wants to move on now," replied Randal, ignoring Roxanne's question.

"To eternity? Like you said?"

"Yes. She just wants to talk to me today. She wants her family to know who... who..." His words trailed off and he closed his thoughts down.

"To know who?"

"Not who... I got it wrong. She just wants them to know she'll be OK."

"Will she really be OK?"

"I'll help her. She needs a grownup to do that. Now let's go home and don't you worry your pretty little head about it all. You trust me, don't you?"

"More than anyone in the whole wide world."

"Then leave Mistral Sommers to me. I'll make sure she's not upset anymore."

"Oh, I knew you could help her. I'm so glad we came today. Can we go for a pizza now?"

He nodded as he bent down and picked her up. He had switched off his mind to her but had to feel her close to him because she was too precious to let go. He must always keep her safe, because Mistral Sommers had lost her life violently and he needed to find her killer in order for her to move on.

He was not used to this spiritual twist. For once he would not be the original perpetrator. Mistral had been someone else's precious daughter.

Randal's complex sense of poetic justice came to the fore. This deed was more in Carlton's line of righteous business, but Randal's demonic disposition was now aimed at Mistral's slayer, who needed to be named, shamed and charged in order to set her free. And then Randal would have no conscience in usurping the law, by adding the guilty party to his ever-expanding funereal list.

***

There was a dark shadow in Mistral's mind as the wind howled and whistled in affinity with her name. Suddenly the rain shed its hammering deluge over the village streets. The pavements shone as reflected lamplight merged into running water.

Some nearby trees and hedges were battered and defeated by the unceasing storm. Her umbrella struggled to shelter her from the worst of the weather but did little to allay her unease.

She walked quickly and approached the bus shelter with some relief. She was slightly breathless as she stood underneath its beckoning seclusion. *What a night I've picked to go to a party! Still, it'll be worth it!*

Ten minutes ticked slowly by and still no sign of a bus. Another five minutes disappeared, then another. She stamped her feet down hard on the ground in some futile effort to dry her new, brown leather boots, inspecting their pointed toes with impaired concentration. They pinched mercilessly, but at fifteen years old, fashion was far more important than comfort.

She made up her mind to walk the whole way. *If a bus comes then it'll be a welcome bonus.*

Her umbrella enveloped her whole being as it rejected the downpour. She passed some lighted shop windows, minus the temptation to peer in at their goods. The glass fronts appeared to run into each other like electric rainbows as she quickened her pace.

Traffic splashed and flashed by her. A stray dog darted dangerously through the middle of some cars and their horns honked in annoyance and apprehension. She jumped at the noise. Then she saw a lorry hurtling along through the sheets of rain. Mistral averted her gaze as the large vehicle screeched to a juddering halt. When she dared to look, she caught sight of the dog's bedraggled tail vanishing into a side street, and the driver moved gratefully on, with an expression of intense relief.

She carried on battling against the elements. An eerie-looking vagrant walked aimlessly ahead of her. As she passed him, he leered at her through red-rimmed eyes, stroking his mangy beard and mumbling to himself. He was drenched, windswept and demented, but she still smiled weakly at his toady attention, trying hard to conceal her anxiety.

She realised that she had now reached the halfway mark of her quest and not one single bus had passed her along the way. She turned off the main road to cut through a back alley that would shorten her journey.

The cold, dark walls had a sinister life of their own. The wind whipped up the falling leaves, and raindrops cascaded in between crumbling bricks and glistening moss.

Cobblestones penetrated the soles of her aching feet and left their unwelcome impression. All the houses seemed alarmingly distant, even though faint cooking smells lingered, hanging on to the dank night air before being washed away by the remorseless wind and rain.

Mistral fought even harder with her umbrella, as the wind whistled its favourite tune and blasted every movable object out of its determined path. It reminded her of an unyielding symphony, an atmospheric brass section carried on a tempestuous current of air.

She stumbled and her boot made contact with an unseen obstacle. The 'thing' squealed loudly and she looked down to see the stray dog that had managed to dodge the traffic beforehand. It hopped towards the wall and lay down to lick its injured paw. Its coat was saturated, the sopping-wet fur plastered to its thin frame.

I thought it was only cats that had nine lives!

Some of the houses that backed on to the alleyway were lit up, allowing the drizzled rays of light to travel down their rear yards and over the passage walls.

The whites of the injured dog's eyes glinted in the fuzzy luminosity as it observed her accusingly. She felt guilty and bent down to offer some comfort, but it growled and barred its teeth menacingly. She stiffened, and as if to add to the drama, a bolt of sheet lightning streaked across the inky sky. The dog flinched and limped away to find another canine haven.

Mistral breathed a sigh of relief, but it was short-lived as the thunder rumbled and rolled overhead. Pulling herself together, she moved on. The cobblestones gave way to a gravel path. She thought she heard a sound behind her and looked back.

She saw nothing except the shadows of fear.

She walked on and caught the same noise again, like crunchy, uneven footsteps in the snow. Her heartbeat quickened along with her strides. The unnerving paces moved nearer, slurring along the small, rounded stones in some absurd dragging motion.

Fear swept through her. Sweat beads trickled down her back and clung to her top lip. She started to run. The unending alley walls swam past her in a nightmarish scenario, their ageing bricks alive with chilled enthusiasm. Her heart thumped wildly inside her ribs and the straggling weeds seemed to suck her under, as the endless wind and rain bent her umbrella to their relentless will.

She ran faster and the being behind her copied her style. Her breathing was heavy and her legs a moving dead weight. Her fashionable, three-inch stiletto heels were hampering her speed as they wobbled and scraped across the rough path. Another fresh gust of wind blew her umbrella inside out and snatched it away. Mistral watched helplessly as it embraced the stormy sky on a pocket of blustering air.

She yanked her head round and saw the outline of a man. Could it be the tramp? The dissolute vagrant she had passed at the start of her foolish excursion? His silhouette drew nearer and called out her name in a vaguely familiar, rasping voice.

Her frozen tongue stuck to the roof of her mouth as terror overcame her. She stumbled, twisting her ankle, wincing with the pain. Her flight was now hampered by injury, but then horror replaced her discomfort as her unsavoury stalker grappled with her from behind. She struggled and screamed, but he smothered her mouth with his leather-gloved hand.

Then everything went black.

Mistral woke up. She was lying on the sopping-wet ground, completely alone. The wind howled and the rain poured as she tried to remember what had happened, but it was all a blank.

She stood up and glimpsed the neon lights ahead. She headed for the main road and saw an approaching bus emerging like a beacon of light through the storm.

She ran to the stop, where another woman was waiting. The bus charged towards them then juddered to a halt. They both stepped onto the platform and into the subsequent warmth and safety.

The driver made some remark about it being rather warm weather for the time of year, but he ignored Mistral as she fumbled in her pocket for her purse.

"I want to go to Willow Road. It's the stop outside the school. How much?" she asked him, but the bus had already moved on and he was still ignoring her.

"How much to Willow Road, please?" she reiterated, but he carried on driving.

"Well, if you don't want my money then!" she snapped, as she studied his profile.

His ears were large and flat, and his lips puckered as he whistled a popular tune.

How strange, uttered Mistral to herself.

She made her way down the aisle to a vacant seat. All the other passengers were dry and oddly untouched by the weather.

No umbrellas either! Nobody seems to notice me at all.

In contrast, her hair was wet and wild, and had dripped all over the shoulders of her leather jacket. Mascara ran down both cheeks, making her warm, brown eyes look like two black smudges on either side of her pretty face. Her lipstick was smeared and distorted the natural shape of her mouth.

She slumped against the windowpane, looking for the driving rain which should be splattering against the glass, making visibility of the outside world blurred.

There's no sign of it. Where is it?

It was all so vague and yet so familiar. She closed her eyes and concentrated while she tried to remember.

Two women were gossiping behind her, their constant chatter interrupting her thoughts. She tried to block out their conversation, but her temples throbbed. Her concentration waned as she heard their unwanted prattle.

"It was a terrible tragedy," said the woman in the navy coat. "Who'd have thought such a thing could happen here? I remember it well, because it was my son's twenty-first birthday. Ten years ago, tonight. The weather was dreadful with nonstop rain and gales."

"It was horrific! Police all over the place, not to mention the news on the telly, and in the papers," replied her companion.

"She was only fifteen. Fifteen! I still don't think she should have been out on her own. Fancy cutting through the back alley. It was just asking for trouble."

"I agree! Apparently, she was on her way to her school. Some of her friends had broken into the gym and were having a party without anyone's consent. Her parents didn't even know she'd gone out! They never found her killer. Poor little Mistral. Such a beautiful girl with an unusual name."

Mistral's head jerked round. Both of the women were still talking but looked straight through her. An image blazed into her brain and then collided with another. Flashback after flashback filtered through her mind in three-dimensional vision.

The wind, the rain, the bus stop, the stray dog, the tramp, the back alley, the dog again, the umbrella, the footsteps, the stalker, the rasping voice and then oblivion.

And now I'm trapped between two dimensions. And my killer was never found. I can't break the cycle of these haunted trips in the storm, every year on the anniversary of my death.

I need someone who can see me or hear my voice. The little girl with the red hair at my old school. She sees me but can't help. But the tall man who came back with her can.

He's very powerful. He's her father and he heard me, but he didn't want to upset his little girl, even though she's aware of me.

And now he'll avenge my death and find the man who murdered me, and then kill him to free me from this curse.

Yes. That's what he said. He spoke to my mind. He told me that he'd help. And he wants poetic justice for me.

His name's Randal Forbes. Yes. That's him. Help me, Randal Forbes. Don't forget your promise.

6

Randal could not get Mistral Sommers out of his head. She invaded his thoughts and blasted away all retaliation towards the other intruders. They would have to wait for their punishment because her desperate spirit needed to move on in order to acquire salvation.

In his quest to free her from her ghostly chains, it never once crossed his mind that his victims, who had also died horribly, specifically the three Haynes children who had drowned, could, in turn, be roaming the earth in spiritual agitation. They simply did not figure in his plans or conscience.

Mistral's killer was now his number-one project of displacement.

He sat at his new computer and searched for her name. A few sites of interest were thrown up, but one main news item caught his immediate attention. He opened up the link and Mistral's picture looked back at him, together with the details of her murder. As soon as he saw her pretty face, he remembered who she was.

It all happened in a freak storm in April 1982. It was big news and was still an unsolved case. The search for her assassin had been watered down, another unresolved statistic in a file.

Randal had been absorbed in his many projects, mostly abroad, at that time.

Randal's slate-grey gaze studied her features until her photograph became alive, not just a flat image on the screen. He took a deep breath and stared into her eyes until his own began to glow with intrusive intent. He traced the outline of her face and his long fingers lingered around her temples.

A dark back alley flashed into his head and he felt the sensation of wind and rain through his hair. He saw her running and struggling with her umbrella. Then he heard the sound of footsteps behind her.

The vision was so vivid that he may as well have turned the clock back ten years and been present in the pathway with her. As she battled against the elements, Randal moved beside her and could hear the sound of the unnerving gait drawing even closer.

Then, a man, smelling strongly of alcohol, called out her name as he grappled with her from behind. He put his hand over her mouth and wrapped his scarf around her neck, pulling it tightly until she could not breathe. She fell to the ground and he kneeled beside her, all the time drawing the broad band closer and tighter around her slender throat, until she stopped breathing altogether.

Randal watched the sickening scene through burning eyes.

The man spoke, as the wind whistled through his greasy hair. "Mistral. My little Mistral. Disobeying your parents again. Sneaking out of the house to your secret party, made up and looking older, so that some spotty boy will feel the need to put his hands all over you. I have to stop you being used and abused because you'll always be my little Mistral. My brother's child. My beautiful niece. My gorgeous girl with the long chestnut hair. You'll be forever young and totally innocent. Oh, so totally innocent now, for your Uncle Reggie."

Randal fumed and felt utterly helpless as Mistral's uncle kneeled down beside her, kissed her cheek, then abandoned her on the sopping-wet ground. Randal saw him disappear out of sight through the pouring rain, battling against the relentless wind.

He looked at Mistral's inert body, soaked and lifeless. He had the overwhelming urge to bring her back, but even he could not create that revival. She had been dead for ten years now and he had just telepathically witnessed her murder.

He pulled himself out of his vision. Now he had a name. Reggie! An uncle on her paternal side of the family. He focused even harder and typed in Reggie Sommers. Nothing.

Hang on! His full name must be Reginald.

He punched in the amended version.

Bingo! One Reginald Sommers, and he's still living in the same locality with his wife and family.

Randal noted his address then looked him up in the phone book. He found the number quite easily and called him.

"Hello? Can I help you?" a female voice requested.

"Yes, hello. May I speak to Reggie, please?" asked Randal in a pleasant tone.

"Just a minute, I'll get him for you. Is it work again?"

"Yes. Just a little question I need to ask him, you know," lied Randal.

"Reggie! It's for you; another problem at work," she shouted across the room.

He cursed then walked to the phone, sighing deeply. It was his day off and he had wanted to relax.

"Hello, what's the matter now?"

"Are you Reggie Sommers?" enquired Randal in a tight voice.

"Yes, who's this, please?"

"Are you Mistral Sommers' uncle?"

There was a long silence.

"Who wants to know?" replied Reggie eventually, in a suspicious tone.

"My names unimportant. I'm calling on behalf of your niece. You see, I know what you did. I know what you did and I'm coming to get you!"

Another long silence and then a frightened answer. "Who the hell is this? You're insane!"

"No! I'm not! But *you* are! You killed her and left her to die alone in the wind and the rain! I saw you! You stalked her as soon as she left the house, and then followed her down that back alley! You wore black leather gloves and I even know the colour of your scarf! It was dark blue with thin green stripes. And you strangled her with it! Didn't you? Then you walked away, knowing full well she was dead!" exclaimed Randal.

Reggie began to breathe very heavily. He could not muster up a reply.

"Are you still there, you perverted creep? You piece of unhinged filth! Now, this is what I want you to do."

Randal entered his brain instantly and effectively. He had a mental image of him, vivid enough for him to invade.

You're going to confess. You'll tell the police, how, and why, you murdered her. You'll say that you've hidden it for ten years. You'll admit that you can't carry on with the guilt of your crime. Now, do this right away! Do you understand? You gutless, nauseating scumbag!

"I understand," replied Reggie mechanically.

When I put down the phone, you won't remember this conversation, just an overpowering compulsion to confess to the police and your family. So, on with your coat and get yourself down to the nearest constabulary, and tell them what a disgusting, squalid piece of pollution you really are. Understood? Uncle Reggie!

"Understood."

On your impure way then. Tatty-bye, teenage-slayer!

***

119

Over the next few days, the newspapers were crammed full of Reginald Sommer's shocking confession. His photograph dominated the headlines and his family were decimated by his act of mutilation.

Randal entered his head again through his picture and spoke to him telepathically in his prison cell.

Hello, Uncle Reggie. How gutless are you today? Well, now I want you to get your just desserts. You vulgar, perverted riff-raff.

So, take the sheet off your bed and fold it over and over again, until it's just one long, narrow strip. Done that? Goody. Now wrap it round your ugly, scraggy neck. Wind it round and round until it feels really tight. Now strangle yourself with it! Just like you did to Mistral. Tighter than tight! Until you can't breathe!

Reginald began to choke but was relentless in his reaction to the vocal command in his head. He was asphyxiating but his hands still pulled the elongated sheet round his throat to the point of total suffocation. His face turned blue, but he was still wrestling with the stretched cloth until he stopped breathing altogether.

And now the circle's complete and Mistral can move on. She can find the peace she so rightly deserves, after ten years of torment.

Go forward, Mistral. Your killer has been named, shamed and removed. He wasn't worthy to kiss your new brown leather boots. Rest in peace, you precious soul.

Randal walked through the patio doors and lit up a cheroot. He saw Roxanne playing in the garden with Amber and called to her. She ran over to him with her skipping rope still in her hand.

"Just thought I'd tell you, pumpkin, that Mistral's very happy now and you won't be seeing her again. I promise." He smiled his special smile.

"Oh, I knew you'd help her, Daddy. I just knew." She grinned and hugged him.

"Go play now," he said softly, and watched her skip down the garden path.

He was about to turn back when suddenly Mistral appeared in front of him, for his eyes only. She beamed and blew him a kiss. Her hair and clothes were bone-dry.

Thank you so much. I can rest now. Forever.

You're welcome. That's all I wanted for you.

Goodbye, Randal Forbes. I'll never forget you.

Ditto, sweet child.

She was still smiling as she disappeared into thin air. Randal nodded. Now he could get back to all of his other pressing major plans of extinction.

***

Hadleigh Masterson chewed the end of his pen and stared into nowhere. He had to complete an important editorial article, but his brain was redundant.

He could not believe what had happened to photographer Elvis Ford and even more so the shocking and instantaneous death of his wife. In a hospital corridor of all places. On the floor. In front of everyone, after visiting her husband and being very vocal about her objection to his consultant's wishes, to transfer him to a mental health unit.

At least that was the explanation given by Dr Winston Ramsey in the newspapers, including the *Daily Announcer.*

Hadleigh recalled that Winston was one of a team of specialists who had witnessed the incredible resurrection of Clive Hargreaves and was mentioned in the numerous press articles at that particular time. In fact, he had spoken personally to him and the other consultants about it all.

It caused quite a stir of publicity for both Clive and the hospital, but there was another witness who had vigorously objected to the sensationalism, more than anybody else. One disgruntled, obsessively private man. Randal Forbes!

Hadleigh felt an alien tremor steal into the nape of his neck and down his spinal cord. His stomach fluttered with what felt like an invasion of deranged butterflies, in an interconnecting arrangement of crooked lines.

There was something very odd going on.

He had not imagined the dazzling light in Randal's uncanny eyes. Elvis had dropped to his knees and then collapsed with both hands clamped around his ears, as if he needed to block out some unbearable sound but failed in the process. In the midst of all his torture he'd began to have what appeared to be an epileptic fit.

Then, Roxanne had fastened her glowing, penetrative gaze on the camera and tape recorder, and they had both exploded in a twin detonation.

Hadleigh lit up a second cigarette in five minutes. He had stopped smoking a while ago, but this present paranormal puzzle had made him kick-start the habit again.

Er, hello? Excuse me, but what the hell did I see? Something exceptionally weird, for sure.

"Honestly, Hadleigh, you're beginning to smell like a chimney. It's really horrible," complained his fiancée Tanya.

"I can't help it. I'm a bag of bloody nerves!"

"Over what?"

"Randal Forbes! That's over what!"

"Randal Forbes? You mean *the* Randal Forbes, sex-God in human form?" she almost swooned.

"If you like," he huffed, feeling jealous regardless of the nightmarish situation.

"So, what has the delectable Mr Forbes done to start you chain-smoking again?"

"Delectable? I don't think so! I used to think so. I idolised him from a distance, in a purely creative sense, as you know. But now? Well, I'm not so sure," he groaned. His hand trembled as he dragged hard on the filter tip.

"What's the problem, Hadleigh? Why has he upset you so

much? This isn't like you at all. You're normally so confident and totally focused."

"I think that Randal Forbes has got supernatural powers. He doesn't just create things with that theme. I think he actually possesses the same authority."

"What! What makes you think that? It's bizarre!" she responded in a disbelieving tone.

"Oh, it's bizarre alright. That's the word. At first, I doubted it, or perhaps didn't want to believe it, but now I'm positive that he's fiercely telepathic. In fact, I think he's an occultist. His whole aura's very dark. Look, Tanya, there's something else. I didn't want to tell you this, but now you've asked, well, I feel that I should."

"Hadleigh, you're freaking me out. I need to know what's going on with you, so please explain," she pleaded, stroking the side of his flushed cheek.

Hadleigh took a deep breath.

How to make this sound real and not like some Hammer horror production?

"Well, here's the thing. Randal sent a car for me to meet up with him for an exclusive interview in the privacy of his own home. I took the freelance photographer Elvis Ford with me."

"Yes, I know that. You were ecstatic," she reminded him. "You talked about nothing else for a week."

"I did. But it began badly and ended up a complete catastrophe. Randal was initially annoyed when he saw Elvis because he'd stipulated no family photos, but I reminded him that he'd agreed to some of himself. Right from the start he behaved as if our presence was a mistake. He was very prickly, cutting and downright rude, especially to Elvis."

Hadleigh hesitated slightly before he continued. "Halfway through the interview, his daughter Roxanne appeared out of nowhere. Randal was very angry that she'd answered a question which was directed at himself. She became most upset with his obvious displeasure. Worse still, Elvis made a massive mistake and photographed her in tears. Randal went ballistic! I swear I'm not exaggerating! His eyes began to glow like two floodlights in the dark. Talk about the Village of the Damned! He never took those eyes off Elvis for one second and he collapsed, then had an epileptic fit."

"Randal's eyes glowed! Are you sure?" asked Tanya disbelievingly.

"Oh, I'm very sure. But there's more to the story!"

"More?"

"Yes, more! Listen very carefully to me. Roxanne focused her own blazing gaze on his camera and my tape recorder. Guess what? They both blew up! I swear they exploded into a thousand pieces! I was so shocked that I lost my balance, banged my head on a coffee table and passed out briefly. When I came round, Elvis was still having a fit and Randal looked like he couldn't give a toss. I can't get the expression in his eyes out of my mind! He looked demonic. And so did his daughter!"

"Demonic? What on earth do you mean?"

"If you'll let me finish, please!"

Tanya's eyes widened. "There's no need to get irritable with me. I've never seen you react like this to anything else. I'm trying to understand."

"Well, understand this! Elvis's wife threatened to take *The Announcer* to the cleaners if I didn't tell her what had happened, as he's still hospitalised in a really bad way."

"Has she started legal proceedings? Is that why you're so… so fired up?"

"Fired up? Fired up! Just listen to the rest of this horror story. Mrs Ford had the same kind of fit as Elvis when she was visiting him! Except she died on the fucking hospital floor! Apparently, she was really upset with Dr Ramsey, who wanted to transfer Elvis to a psychiatric unit. Incidentally, he's the very same doctor who witnessed Clive Hargreaves' mind-blowing recovery with Randal in the room. Randal in the thick of it once more! He's like some kind of bad omen!"

Hadleigh paused for breath then continued as Tanya stared at him disbelievingly. "Getting back to Gemma Ford's death, well, Dr Ramsey tried to save her, but he couldn't revive her. So, she snuffed it! What I'm saying, Tanya, is that Randal's *always* at the centre of these weirder than weird circumstances. I seriously believe that he has an uncontrollable dark side lurking behind his charismatic aura. I don't know what it is exactly, but I'm sure it's there, and he taps into it whenever he feels wronged or angry. And so does his daughter, even though she's adopted. Now that's even weirder, don't you think?"

Tanya's expression was one of total scepticism as she spoke. "Oh, Hadleigh! There must be a feasible explanation to all of this! Had you been drinking? I've seen Randal on the telly many times. He's gorgeous, so ridiculously charming with a very appealing smile. He's one half of one of the most celebrated couples on the planet. You mean to tell me that Alison Forbes married a warlock? So, what does that make her? Head witch of the Weybridge coven with a cauldron bubbling on the hob for like-minded visitors?" she quipped, but the fun was totally lost on Hadleigh's concerned reaction.

"Tanya, wise up! I'm telling you that there's something bad going on! He makes my skin crawl and so does his daughter, even though she's just a child. When his eyes flash, they render Dracula ineffective! You weren't there!"

"I'm not saying that you imagined it all. I'm just thinking that there's got to be a practical answer to what you thought you saw," she reasoned.

"A practical answer? I often see glowing eyes followed by an epileptic fit! I mean, it's practically commonplace! And while we're at it, let's throw in an exploding camera and tape recorder for good measure, also at the end of a radioactive gaze! Oh, and just for extras, let's include a similar but fatal fit for the wife of the injured party who was threatening legal action. I mean, it's a daily occurrence!" he raved.

"I'm going now, Hadleigh, and when you've calmed down, give me a call," she berated.

"Fine."

"Fine," repeated Tanya as she reached for her jacket. She put it on and gave him a dirty look at she walked out the door.

Hadleigh was breathing very heavily and his head was pounding. He rubbed both temples with his fingers and lit up yet another cigarette. He inhaled deeply and blew out the smoke in a desperate line, trying to steady his erratic heartbeat.

It was Gemma Ford's death that had put the deadly icing on the crumbling cake. Some innate sixth sense told him that Randal had reached out and caused it. It was the perfect solution for him: to rid himself of one irate wife on the verge of blabbing everything to the tabloids and naming Randal in some lurid circumstance that had caused her husband's infirmity. Dragging his name, yet again, through a nasty legal entanglement, with the police and press all over Randal's private life, looking for more answers.

She simply had to go. I'm sure of it, no matter what Tanya thinks.

Intrusion was the last thing Randal needed, especially after all the constant encroachment that seemed to follow him around. Intrusion of the worst kind. A relentless intensity. A veritable infringement of his privacy.

Hadleigh meditated deeply yet again on his much-anticipated but disastrous meeting with Randal.

My exclusive interview was designed to show him in a more inspirational light. It was meant to be an article of unquestionable appreciation, to remind the reader of his unique, original gift for the written word. To guide the people away from all the sensational, unwanted reports of his legal nightmare.

So, what happens? Another dire situation heading towards the law courts! Not a Carlton Flint comatose state but definitely an Elvis Ford injurious posture, acquired in uncommon circumstances, with his wife thrown in as a deceased theatrical extra.

Hadleigh remembered a couple of disturbing facts from his Beaumont College days in Oxford. It happened before his time there, but it was almost folklore.

Both Randal and Clive had been hauled in for questioning over two fatalities: a couple of fellow students who were their mutual friends. Robbie Sterling had fallen over a cliff in Cumbria and died. Marcus Pennington was institutionalised for murder and arson, causing the death of his grandfather, who was a priest. Once again, Randal was in the very epicentre of the fatal earthquake.

In the middle of all his ruminating the telephone rang. He hoped it was Tanya, phoning to apologise. Hadleigh sighed deeply as he picked up the receiver. "Hello, Hadleigh Masterson here, can I help you?"

"Hello, Randal Forbes here, and you most definitely can."

Hadleigh nearly jumped out of his skin. *My God!*

"What c-can I d-do for y-you?" he stuttered, cursing himself for sounding alarmed.

"Well, for a start you can dispense with the stammer. It doesn't suit you and it makes me suspicious."

"Sorry. It's just that I was... I was... well, I was..."

"Thinking of me? How flattering."

Hadleigh was struck dumb. He had never felt so cornered or speechless in the whole of his confident life.

"Now listen very closely, Mr Masterson. Since your photographer's indescribable spouse kicked the banshee bucket, the police have been sniffing around looking for answers. Apparently, she had paid them a venomous visit, pointing her fanatical forefinger in my domesticated direction. In turn, they paid me a most unwanted and unwarranted house call. They had to know why Elvis had left the building, shake, rattle and rolling in the process. So, I told them he was obviously epileptic. A most palatable and self-evident prognosis, don't you think? Are you still there? Are you awake, Mr Masterson? More importantly, am I getting through to you?" asked Randal in a menacing tone.

"Y-yes."

"Good! To continue, the police are going to question you as a witness to the whole tiresome episode. Now, I need to know what you're going to tell them. So, can you fill me in with your stammering statement, if you please?"

"W-when?"

"Now would be a good time," replied Randal sardonically.

"W-what d-do you want me to s-say?"

"Why, the truth, my fellow Beaumonteer! The whole truth, and nothing but the truth. What else did you have in mind?"

"But I can't r-remember anything because I p-passed out."

"Did you now? So, you won't be getting any imaginary *flashbacks*, will you?" asked Randal with emphatic double meaning.

"I saw nothing."

"Now you've got it. That's the tactical ticket. So, can I count on your dependable discretion?"

"W-whatever you w-want."

"What I want, Mr Masterson, is for you to stop ruminating. Your head is cluttered with dangerous deciphering. It's very transparent. Just carry on with your regular reporting and leave me and my family out of your high-handed headlines, because if you don't, then it will be *you* who'll be dominating the front pages of your own proverbial publication. A veritable scoop for your competitors. Is that understood?"

"I... understand."

"I thought you would. Now, be a good little editor and put your fiancée in the proper picture as well."

Hadleigh's eyelashes began to twitch in unison. His head felt poached, like an inedible, violated egg. He could feel Randal

128

ferreting around in his braincells, just waiting to pounce on any suspicious activity.

"I'll d-do whatever you w-want. Just p-please, leave b-both of us alone."

"My pleasure. But a word of warning. If you *ever* employ anyone in the future who takes intrusive photographs of my family, it will be more than a camera and a tape recorder on the receiving end of destruction. Is that clear?"

Hadleigh could not speak.

"I said, is that clear?"

"V-very."

"Good. Have a nice day," concluded Randal, as he put down the phone.

Hadleigh was a quivering wreck. He now knew beyond any shadow of a doubt that Randal was plugged into real dark powers and would have to be avoided at all costs. And that also applied to his daughter Roxanne.

But wait a minute. She's adopted! She's not even related to him! But they look so alike! Oh, lord, for all I know she could have been hatched! Stop analysing and just move away from it all! He's too dangerous! A paranormal panther on the loose, clawing and mauling everything in his intrusive way! To think I was besotted with his genius!

Hadleigh swallowed hard. He needed a stiff drink. He also needed to call Tanya and tell her she was right and that he was mistaken. That way they would both be safe and kept far away from Randal's infernal stare: those disabling, merciless rays of satanic light.

The phone rang again.

"Hello," whispered Hadleigh.

"I'm happy with your reasoning. So, for the moment, you're both safe. Don't make me regret my decision, Mr Masterson," stated Randal firmly, and he put the receiver down before Hadleigh could reply.

Oh my God! Now my thoughts belong to him. He's stolen them and has a hotline to my meditation. How many other heads has he plundered along the way, and to what end?

Hadleigh tried to stop all reasoning, but he suddenly remembered Spencer Forbes' suicide. There had been a rumour circulating that he and Randal were not the best of buddies, let alone cousins. Why else would Spencer have been representing Techscreen, the same company who were countersuing Randal? Just what possessed a successful barrister, in the prime of his life, to jump off a motorway bridge into the line of traffic? Another fatality with Randal centre-stage!

I must stop suspecting. Now isn't the time for speculation. Now is the moment to put all doubts and fears behind me. Forget about Randal Forbes. He doesn't matter anymore.

I'll give away all his books and rid myself of his influence. He doesn't exist. He doesn't exist. He doesn't exist.

The phone rang again. Hadleigh did not want to answer it, but it kept on ringing. He picked up the receiver with a trembling hand. "Hello," he croaked.

"Hadleigh? You still sound upset. I'm so sorry. I shouldn't have been as dismissive. Forgive me," appealed Tanya.

"Nothing to forgive. You were right. I built it up out of all proportion. I'm sorry too."

Back in Weybridge, Randal put Hadleigh's photograph into his drawer of targeted images. He was no threat right now, but the minute he relapsed, he would remove him; effectively, callously and thoroughly. Without hesitation or culpability.

★★★

Dr Winston Ramsey was going over a patient's notes at the end of his clinic when he felt a strange sensation inside his head. It seemed to scratch and scrape at his brain, trying to enforce itself into the deepest mass of living matter, but all it did was remain ineffective and redundant.

He thought he heard a faint string of commands, but he casually dismissed them as unimportant and impervious. So, he just carried on reading his notes and dictated a letter for his secretary to type out later.

Randal was in Astral TV's studio one. He was on his own and incandescent with rage. He had it all planned out, the perfect moment for Winston to respond to his evil bidding. But Winston was having none of it, not even a microscopic bit of it.

Randal's murderous flaming eyes scorched the photograph in his hand as he tried repeatedly to instruct his victim on the joys of self-mutilation. The response was systematically regarded. Purposefully ignored. His destructive mandate bounced back at him in a mocking reverberation of his fatal commandment.

His eyes became two laser beams of incinerating ignition. Winston's picture burst into flames in his hand and nearly charred his fingers. He was livid as he flicked the image into the paper bin and watched it burn.

Who put the narcotic spanner in the Winston works? Who made him the deathless doctor? Let me guess! Carlton 'flaxen-haired' Flint, in his hypnotic element as the blond, blue-eyed, benevolent, biblical blockade! The above-board affectation of 'the gift'. In my way! In Winston Ramsey's head! The interfering inhabitant of his saviour's stronghold.

Fuck you both! You won't escape me! The writings on the whippersnapper wall. I'm reworking the whole script, but the ending is still intact. Just one word. Annihilation!

Randal's eyes were still alight. This was the first time that his telepathic powers had been rejected and most emphatically overlooked. His face was twisted up into an ugly, snarling rearrangement of his well-proportioned features, a monstrous version of his captivating allure. He looked totally demonic with a tortuous, crooked, serpentine expression which snaked across his sinuous face and remained there. It took every morsel of his mastery to pull himself out of his colossal discomposure.

He heard footsteps outside the door. It opened and Dean walked in holding a cup of coffee. "Hey, Rand! You didn't tell me you were coming in today," he enthused, in his usual affectionate manner.

Randal spun round so he was looking the other way. His eyes were still glaring and he could not risk Dean being witness to his watered-down wrath. Even that remained ablaze.

"What's up? Are you OK?" asked Dean to Randal's broad, classical shoulders.

"It's nothing. Just thinking. I had a definite project in mind and tried to bring it to life, but some awkward little gremlin got in the way. My imagination's on strike at the minute. Still, not to worry, there's always tomorrow," he explained, and turned back round to face Dean, his handsome features restored, with just a miniscule glint in his eyes which made him look irresistible as opposed to irascible.

"Oh, that happens to me as well. A total blank page and then boom! Everything falls back into place. Sometimes even better than I originally planned. Maybe the little gremlin came out to play in order for you to devise something even more dynamic," advised Dean.

"Wise words, grasshopper," praised Randal. *Even more than you realise.*

"Did you know that Clive's outside? He's just having a chat to one of the crew, but he wants to talk to you. It's just as well you're here because he needs to speak to you as soon as possible."

"Does he now?" *He suspects I've binned the abominable battleaxe Mrs Elvis Ford and he's wondering who's next.*

"I'll make two more cups of coffee, huh?"

"No sugar in mine." Randal smiled. *You must be kept sweet, though, and so must Clive. So big grin and switch on the seductive sorcery.*

Clive walked into the room at that point, practically colliding with Dean.

"Sorry!" they both apologised together, and then laughed.

"Coffee, Clive?"

"Love one."

Dean patted his shoulder as he left. Clive took off his jacket and sat down in Randal's chair. He lit up a cigarette without talking and stared at him with suspicious eyes.

Randal reached inside the pocket of his favourite brown leather jacket, which was hanging on the back of the chair where Clive was now sitting. He brought out a pack of cheroots and lit one up, all the time saying nothing but taunting Clive with his nearness. He purposefully brushed against him as he made his way to the door.

"Where do you think you're going?" asked Clive in a tight voice.

"Where would you like me to go?"

"Nowhere. I'd like you to stay."

"Would you now? Well then, how can I resist?" provoked Randal, as he pulled up a chair to sit down directly opposite Clive, staring at him through a haze of tobacco smoke.

Clive was trying hard to ignore Randal's screaming sensual proximity, especially the magnetic expression in his narrow gaze. He cleared his throat to speak. "Why did you kill Gemma Ford?" asked Clive without hesitation.

"Who?"

"You know exactly who I mean, so stop acting the goat."

"Ah, the goat! According to the Zodiac, my sun sign is Capricorn, represented by none other than 'the goat'. So, surely, Clive, that gives me carte blanche to act as I wish to with the aforementioned creature?"

"Stop it! Just stop it! I asked you a valid question! Why the hell are you wasting valuable psychic energy on another unfeeling, pointless removal? It's bad enough that her husband's permanently deranged! Did you also have to get rid of his caring wife?"

"Caring wife? Is that what she was? I'd say more like the Witch of Eastwick on helium. The 'caring wife' sent the police round to our house, filling their heads with a suspicious scenario of events. More intrusion and a probable lawsuit. Alison and the kids were upset for days afterwards. She needed to disappear. Banshee bitch!" snarled Randal.

"You didn't have to kill her! Warming up behind her photograph and then taking her over, making her choke!"

"I didn't have her photograph. I was there at the hospital. On the spot. It was almost orgasmic."

"On the spot! Are you crazy? Anyone could have recognised you! How stupid was that!" chastised Clive.

"I was in disguise. Even I didn't recognise me. I did it all behind a newspaper, pretending to read. It was very quick. She didn't suffer for long. More's the pity."

"Oh, well, that's all right then!"

"I'm so glad you agree."

"Who's next? I mean, you're on a Randal-roll. Do you realise how much I worry about each crime? Worry in case it drains you altogether. Worry in the event that one day you'll be found out. Worry about Roxanne and her inheritance. Worry about relapsing again with the anxiety. Why can't you just hypnotise them into another way of looking at the situation? I know you've the power, so why kill them all off?" beseeched Clive.

"Calm down, Clive. You'll burst your benevolent bubble. You're getting steamed up over nothing. I'm OK. You're OK. Roxanne's OK. We're all OK. I always win."

"You've not exactly answered my question," he urged.

"Which one? I've lost count."

"Hypnosis! Why don't you do it? Like you wiped Marcus's memory away so that he wouldn't remember anything bad about you? Not that I condone one tiny bit of that epic production. Especially now that he thinks you're some kind of erotic angel, visiting him and making him feel special, when all the time you're playing a dangerous, spiteful game of 'if only you knew what I did to you, and your grandfather, and I'm still screwing your wayward mother in her four-poster bed!'. That hypnosis is totally corrupt, but you could turn it all round and apply a more orderly version of it in the future, for any suspecting so-called lesser mortals!" admonished Clive.

Randal pulled his chair even closer to Clive so that they were practically face to face. "Have you finished? I always win. Losing is not in my dictionary. I know what I'm doing. I'm the true recipient of 'the gift' and this is the way it has to be enacted: a complete and utter removal for any suspicious lesser mortal who gets too near its source. Hypnosis is a side-line, not a solution. There are no half-measures. I don't, and won't, leave things half-undone. I have to tie up all the loose ends, and if that means another fatality, then so be it. I appreciate your concern, but it's misplaced and intrusive. So just take a step back, Clive, and chill out. It's all cool. All of it," clarified Randal with glittering eyes.

Clive sighed deeply and then continued. "One day, one dark day you'll come unstuck, and where will that leave us all? Not just me, but everyone who worships you. Alison and your children, especially Roxanne. Your parents, your deluded Uncle Ashley, your sister Patricia, your aunts. And there's Dean. Oh my word, Dean, who idolises you. All your disciples who adore you. Because we all do, you know. The true ones. The ones who know you and the ones who think they do. We're all affected and infected. One way or another. What would we all do if you... if you slipped up, and left us alone? Don't you yell at me, Randal Forbes! Don't you dare yell at me!" expounded Clive passionately.

Randal felt his genuine concern and spoke softly in return. "I'm not going anywhere. You've got me for this life and beyond. Clive, please! Stop all the negativity, because that's all it is. Your negative thoughts. They're taking you over and making you ill when there's absolutely no need. No reason at all."

"Carlton Flint's on your case now. He's after your crown. He means to destroy you and uncover your crimes. He wants you relegated behind bars, banged up for your homicidal sins in a judicial sense. He's powerful, and don't underestimate his capabilities. He's bounced back at full throttle and he's spoiling for a winning fight."

"The starman's a first. I'll grant you that one. But I'll find a way to defeat him. I promise you, Clive. Whatever he has in mind for me will not stop me from halting him."

"Why can't the pair of you just call it quits?" he groaned.

"You know why. Like you said, he's spoiling for domination. There's too much water under the blasphemous bridge. He's the anointed one and I'm the rogue angel. He wants to send me down, legally and spiritually. I'm ready for him, but I need your support, not your doubts and distrust. You're the designated protector of 'the gift'. So, start shielding it, defending it and sheltering it. But most of all, champion it!

Clive nodded and agreed, but Randal saw the shadows under his eyes.

He's got a right to be worried about me. Flint's a formidable challenge. He's already bed-blocked Dr Ramsey's braincells against my plan of elimination, but I'll derail his good intentions.

And, in the end, I'll be the victor and blast this holier-than-thou imposter, together with his consecrated interpretation, into the burning fires of hell.

With no way out. And no way back!

7

Francine Flint had finished her lunch and was browsing through some recipes in the kitchen when she felt an incursion inhabiting her inner thoughts. It was primarily daunting but then she quickly adapted to its residency. She stopped reading and sat up ramrod-straight in her chair, as she focused on the command in her head. She was totally in tune with the hypnotic voice.

Francine, I need to see you. I want you to meet me this afternoon at three o'clock precisely. I'm at the Abbey Hotel, Orange Grove, in your town centre. I'll be waiting for you in room 34, so just come straight up and don't reveal to anyone where you're going. Tell Carlton that you need some extra shopping and act normally. You mustn't give him reason to question anything. When you see me, I'll be wearing jeans, a white T-shirt and a blue velvet jacket. You don't know who I am, but it's imperative that you come. I won't take up too much of your time. See you soon. Be discreet and don't be late.

Francine felt compelled to meet the owner of the voice. She did not have a clue who he was, but it did not seem to matter. The only thing that concerned her was to be on time for him, that she must be there at three o'clock, not one second before or afterwards.

She looked at her watch. It was nearly one-thirty, so she began to prepare for her clandestine encounter. She needed to freshen up and change her clothes.

Carlton was reading the newspaper when he heard Francine running up the stairs. He wondered what the hurry was. "Francine? Are you OK?"

"Fine. I just remembered some shopping I need for a new recipe. I want to get there before they sell out of fresh produce," she explained from the top step, in a casual manner.

Carlton shook his head and smiled. His wife and her recipes were a regular occurrence. She was always happy in the kitchen experimenting with new dishes.

In no time at all she descended the stairs and picked up her car keys.

"I won't be long," she said from the hallway.

"No need to rush," replied Carlton warmly.

She got into the car, drove down the driveway and then set off with a determination born out of the hypnotic voice in her head.

★★★

Randal lit up a cheroot in room 34 of the exclusive hotel. He looked like a dangerous, seductive predator on the psychic prowl.

He inhaled deeply, blew out the smoke and laughed to himself, as he mulled over his next preliminary project of magical mayhem.

It all hinged on this first necessary meeting with Francine. He could have easily spoken to her mind and asked her to do his bidding without a face-to-face assemblage, but his cruel, hard-hearted, ruthless sense of drama had come out to frolic. He embraced it in order to make absolutely sure of her full attention, without the remotest possibility of Carlton's suspicion.

Gazing at her photograph in his hand, he had already wiped Francine's memory of him right out of her mind so that she would have no recognition of his voice, name or celebrity. All she would see and hear was his unknown face and his crucial 'well-meaning' advice.

He looked at his Rolex Daytona watch. Not long to go now. He observed the second hand moving round the dial, one tick at a time. *Here we go then: five, four, three, two, one, lift-off!*

Francine knocked twice, but Randal's grip was already on the door handle. He opened it wide. "Francine! You look so beautiful. Please, come in," he appealed, with the most disarming smile.

She held her breath at his suffocating presence and he could hardly contain his glee at the fact.

"Who are you? You're so handsome! I need to see you, but I'm not sure why," she replied robotically.

"Please sit here with me while I explain." He spoke softly, wooing her towards the edge of the bed with his charming demeanour that hid a treacherous, deceitful streak of spiteful intent.

She did as he said and then stared at him, waiting for an explanation. He gathered his thoughts together and spoke. "This is not an easy thing for me to tell you, but I wanted complete privacy so I could alert you to the facts. I think you have an absolute right to know the truth. To learn what your husband has in mind for you."

"Oh?" she queried, batting her long eyelashes and crossing her shapely legs.

Randal smiled to himself. He was relishing every moment. "Francine. Listen closely to me. Carlton wants to kill you. He's taken out a life insurance policy in your name which will pay out thousands of pounds if you should die before him. I know he has money, lots of revenue, but he's a very avaricious man and can never have enough. Also, far more treacherously, he's been having a long-term affair with your best friend. They plan to be together after your death. I'm so sorry, but you have to know all of this."

Randal watched her facial expression as his lies sank in.

"Carlton wants to kill me? He's having an affair with Stella? But what should I do? I really don't know what to do. Will you help me?" she requested, completely accepting Randal's explanation calmly without asking any other valid questions.

He looked intently into her desirable brown eyes. She was quite a catch. He could have her at the click of his fingers. He felt aroused, but he needed to concentrate on the real reason he had brought her here.

"What you do is this. You have to kill *him* before he murders *you*. His plan is evil. It's the worst crime and he should be punished before he even tries. Your friend Stella also needs to die. The pair of them are poison."

"But how do I kill them?" she enquired in a totally agreeable tone.

"I'll help you with that. I want you to remember this one word, and when you hear it in your head, you'll automatically do exactly what I tell you to do."

"What word is that, please?" she enquired casually.

"Intrusion."

"Intrusion?"

"Yes, intrusion. When you hear that word, you'll obey my orders and carry them out without hesitation."

"Without hesitation," she repeated, twirling a lock of her long dark hair around her finger, aware of Randal's sexy, charismatic aura, regardless of her hypnotic state.

"Now, Francine, I want you to go back home and forget you saw me today," he said, leaning forward and stroking her soft cheek. "Will you do that? Just for me? Hmm? Tell me that you will."

"I'll do that. Just for you," she complied.

I wonder what else you'd do for me under different circumstances. You need to get home before your insufferable husband picks up on any suspicious vibes. You see, he could easily slip inside my head just as I could willingly slip inside you. A double meaning if ever I heard one. Hell, I'm so hard.

"I'll be in touch, Francine. Don't forget the password. I can only help you if you recognise it. What is it?"

"Intrusion. I won't forget it."

"Good girl. Now pick up some fresh produce, drive home and carry on with your new recipe."

"I will. Goodbye, and thank you. What's your name?" she asked mechanically with a robotic expression.

"My name? You don't need to know, but because you're so beautiful and agreeable, I'll tell you. They call me the Scarlet Pimpernel."

"The Scarlet Pimpernel," she repeated with glazed eyes.

"That's me, sweetheart."

Francine licked her glossy lips and Randal's erection began to throb. He needed to relieve himself and she was his for the taking. He was more than tempted.

"Why don't you lie down on the bed with me?" he requested impulsively.

"I thought you wanted me to go home."

"That can wait a little longer."

His passion communicated itself to her hypnotised state. He began to undress and told Francine to do the same.

"Just leave your panties on for me, and I'll stay in my briefs. Let's take it slowly," he breathed heavily.

She did as he asked and they lay side by side. He kissed her passionately, stroking her shapely bottom. Then he manipulated her breasts, pinching the hard nipples. He pressed up against her, rubbing his pulsating bulge against her silk panties, putting his hand inside them to finger her wet vagina. Then he guided her hand into his underwear to release his enormous joystick, which was already leaking at the tip.

"Hell, I need to come," he groaned. "I must control it, my angel, because I want to play with you."

He bent down to her left breast, took the swollen, hard nipple into his mouth and sucked it. Then he did the same to the other one.

"Oh, Scarlet Pimpernel," moaned Francine, as she took off her panties. He mounted her and she wrapped both legs around his hips.

"Are you on the pill?" he asked in a thick voice.

"Pill?"

"Yes, the birth-control pill?"

"No. I'm not," she panted.

"Damn it."

He held his pulsating manhood in his own hand and slid it backward and forward against the opening of her vaginal lips, all the time whispering lustful endearments.

"I'm going to shoot in between your legs. I can't come inside you and take a chance without a condom. Francine Flint, do you know how irresistible you are?"

Randal removed his underwear so he was naked and she could feel the full effect against her satin skin.

"Here it comes! I'm going to explode!"

A fountain of sperm spurted uncontrollably all over her and the look of painful ecstasy on his face caused Francine to have a prolonged orgasm. She squealed with delight.

"Well, Mrs Flint, did that please you? My only regret is that I didn't come inside you, but we couldn't take the chance, could we?" he rasped.

"Oh, that would have been so good!"

"Mind you, we can always do it again. I'll pull out just before I come. It was too urgent before. But I'm ready to try, if you are?"

"Oh, yes, please."

"You're a firecracker, aren't you?"

"I am with you."

"What about with Carlton? Is he well-endowed? I've been told that I'm pretty huge in that area. Do you think you'll be able to accommodate me?"

"He's not as big as you, but he's still good," she purred.

"Is he now?"

He kissed her shapely mouth and caressed her whole length with long, drawn-out strokes, expertly demonstrating the Randal-effect, from her head to her curled-up toes. Then his mouth followed the same trail for fifteen minutes.

"Play with me," he almost begged, directing her hand towards his eternal erection.

He groaned as she massaged his manhood, gently squeezing his engorged testicles in a circular motion, causing the heat to intensify along the whole length.

"Sit on me," he instructed, his voice cracking with lust.

Francine sat up and slid down on him. She felt his hot, pulsating member deep inside her. He reached up and put both hands on her soft breasts, toying with them both as he lunged into her womanhood.

"Can you feel it? I'm on fire for you," he almost growled.

"Oh, yes. That's so good!"

"Bounce on it! Come on, Mrs Flint. Move your body like you've never done before with anyone else."

Francine flung herself into action and Randal's eight-inch pleasure dome penetrated deeply inside her.

"Come with me," he begged as he pushed and jerked.

"Oh, I will," she complied, and she felt him grow even harder.

"Nearly there now. Stop bouncing. I'm pulling out. Ooh! It won't stop! So much juice! You're so sexy! What have you done to me? I've soaked you! Again! Ooh!"

"Oh, Scarlet Pimpernel, that was so good," she said breathlessly, as she rolled over on to her back.

Randal sat up and inspected her naked form. She was absolutely covered in his sperm. Her breasts were huge and soft, the nipples still erect from his fondling. He groaned because he still wanted her, regardless of the intensity of his former orgasms.

He lay down on top of her and his tongue traced the shapely outline of her mouth.

"I want to come in between your breasts. I'm still hard."

"Yes, Scarlet Pimpernel. Yes, please," she almost begged.

The fact that he was taking hypnotic advantage of Carlton Flint's wife was the most massive turn-on. Randal was more aroused momentarily than he had ever been with anyone else. His whole body was on fire and his eyes flashed with passion and lust. His phallus was unceasingly red and erect. He thought it was going to combust.

"Let me lick and suck your nipples first."

He took both, in turn, in his mouth and tugged at the hard tips. He swirled his hot, stiff tongue around each areola, then sucked hard on the swollen buds. He moved up her curvy frame so that his extended member rested just below her breasts.

"Have you any idea how worked up I am, Mrs Flint?" he panted.

"How worked up are you, Scarlet Pimpernel?" she whispered.

"Do you want me to show you?"

"Yes, please."

"Your wish is my command."

He moved even further up her body so that his extended member rested against her face. He held it in his hand and moved the dripping tip across her mouth, outlining the shape of her lips with its throbbing, wet head.

"Suck it for me," he gasped.

Francine obliged, causing him to yell out with rapturous delight. He was too aroused.

"Stop! Stop, Mrs Flint, otherwise I'll come right now!"

He reassembled himself and moved downwards so that his erection rested in between her breasts. He pushed them together so that they smothered his vibrating manhood. He began to vigorously rub up and down, as if his life depended on the desperate movement. At the same time his hand reached down to caress her womanhood.

"Come with me, sexy lady! Oh, fuck!" he yelled, and then shouted even louder as he flooded her breasts with a copious amount of semen, still pushing vigorously after the third eruptive orgasm.

When it was all over, they got washed and dressed, and Francine, still in a Randal-trance, said goodbye. A devilish, cruel smile played around the corners of his shapely mouth. He kissed her passionately before he let her out of the door, then watched her walk gracefully to the lift.

The starman's better half! You won't remember anything that happened today. Sorry, Francine, but he's running out of time, and with your help, I can watch from the side of the spectral stage. So, let the show begin, you desirable, cover girl. I don't believe this! I'm still hard! Incredible! Where's the Vaseline?

★★★

It took Randal some time to drive back to Weybridge. His erection needed to deflate as he was still on an erotic high. When he finally got home, flaccid and relaxed, Roxanne was waiting for him impatiently. He sat down at the table with a cup of coffee and she climbed uninvited on his knee, putting her nose against his, saying nothing out loud but bombarding him telepathically.

Where have you been, Daddy? You promised to take us all out for a pizza today, but you forgot. Why?

I had an important meeting. I'm sorry I forgot. We'll do it again. I promise.

But you promised to take us today. Where did you go? Mummy, Ryan and Amber are in the garden, and they're upset with you. I waited inside for you to come home because I saw you in my head driving the car. Where were you?

She scanned his brain. An undressed pretty lady flashed into her mind. She moved her nose away from his so that she had a better view of his face. Identical eyes locked together. She knew he had met another woman who looked vaguely familiar.

Oh no! Was he with someone else again, making another baby like he did with Maxine?

It's not what you're thinking. He spoke reassuringly to her thoughts.

Promise? You're not seeing another pretty lady instead of Mummy, are you? I'll be very, very, very upset if you are!

No. I love your mummy too much. The lady I saw was part of a plan.
Plan?
Yes. To get rid of the starman.
Oh!

Roxanne's whole body jerked backwards and she nearly fell off him. He grabbed her just in time. She was excited as she jumped up and down on his knee with unrestrained enthusiasm.

How? Tell me! Who is she? What's she going to do? Will she help us? Can I do anything?

Now, don't get over-excited. We don't want anyone else knowing. I'll tell you everything again. This is only the start. Nothing's happened yet.

But why do you need this lady to help? Who is she?

Randal shook his head, shushed her, then put his finger against her lips. Roxanne's eyes glittered with incitement and perception. She rapidly examined his brain with her own inbuilt radiological device and plucked the name of Francine Flint out of his head.

She's the starman's wife! You met the starman's wife! Why?

Randal blocked off his erotic thoughts and just let her hear his present conversation.

146

Like I said, it's only the start of the plan. When there's more to tell you then I will. I've had a long drive home and I don't want any more questions. I've a lot of thinking to do. I've got to make sure of the order of things. Now, be a good little girl and go play in the garden or something. Apologise to them all for me. I'm busy.

Roxanne felt his psychic withdrawal. She saw a mental brick wall. He had locked her out of any more information. She hated it when he did that because she would never do that to him. Everything she had was his for the taking. All her ideas, every thought in her head, all her creations belonged to him. No questions barred. Nothing concealed. Her bottom lip jutted out in the usual reaction to his disengagement.

I don't like it when you leave me out. I'm your special little girl.

Randal tutted as he lifted her off his knee and placed her on the floor. He kissed the top of her head and then walked away towards his study. She had been dismissed.

She watched his long, loose strides as he glided away from her and her eyes filled with frustrated tears. She spoke aloud to the back of his head. "I only want to help, Daddy. I'm a good girl, really."

He turned round to face her, his eyes softening as he looked into her own. "I know, but just for now, the only help I need is to be alone to think things out. I love you and you're my special little girl. Now, go play!" he said lovingly, then disappeared into his room.

Roxanne's heart sang. Warm words and a Randal-smile made the whole world wonderful, magical and alive again.

Then an unbearable elation filtered through her entire body at the thought of her most unequalled, precious father working out a plan to blast the starman out of his galaxy. He would guarantee that everything would be right again. Like it was before Carlton interrupted their majesty, before he had jetsetted into their dominion.

My daddy will make sure that you'll never be in our way again, starman. And I'll be the only other special one with 'the gift'. I tried to kill you, but I messed it up. You hurt me. I flew across the room and banged my head hard, so I really, really wanted you to die from a big bang to your head.

But then you woke up. Why did you wake up? You used 'the gift' and I really don't know why it helped you because you're a bad man. But my daddy won't make a mistake like me. He'll kill you and I won't miss you one little bit. So, stay away and never come back. Ever!

Randal's head was full of lethal ideas. It was just a matter of putting the pieces together like a jinxed jigsaw. He could hear Roxanne's thoughts through the wall. She was placing him in an unquestionable position of supreme domination. She was full of hatred for the imposter, and so was he. It would not be easy, but he owed her this outright victory as the true recipient of 'the gift'. For the future preservation of her inheritance.

★★★

Hadleigh Masterson digested a leading, controversial article in the *Daily Announcer*. He was absolutely horrified at the headlines.

'RANDAL FORBES AND HIS CORRUPT DARK GENIUS!'

It had been written and submitted in his absence by a freelance journalist in order to boost their own career and the paper's readership. How on earth had this piece escaped him? Someone should have run it by him before it had gone to press.

Who the hell's Fletcher Trent? I've never heard of him. I need to speak to this dangerous clown. I shouldn't have taken a break, but I had to get my head together, and now look what's happened! Some clever dick who probably wants my job gets in on the dirty action!

Of all the celebrities to write about on the planet, he had to pick on Randal Forbes! It's inflammatory and defamatory. Randal will be livid and I'm the one on his murderous radar! It more than hints at his attraction to occultist rituals and supernatural abilities, or at least, it strongly implies it. Oh, Lord. I'm dead!

While Hadleigh was trembling with fear, Carlton Flint was oblivious to his terror. His smile grew wider and broader, as he read the same newspaper. His plan had worked beautifully. He had become friendly with Fletcher Trent through their mutual interest in astrology and he had contacted him intentionally with an ulterior motive. As a result, a comprehensive, unflattering article on Randal was definitely in the immediate pipeline.

He had a long meeting with Fletcher, filling his head full of Randalesque psychic allusion. Carlton was told that the editor of *The Announcer* was on indefinite leave due to his connection with the Elvis Ford injurious incident. Also, that Ford's wife, Gemma, had died in mysterious circumstances in the corridor where her husband had been hospitalised. Carlton smelt Randal's satanic scent all over the double atrocity.

Carlton's need to bring Randal down was so strong that he had initially overlooked Fletcher's safety. Subsequently, as a precaution, he had hypnotised him through a photograph to resist any telepathic reaction, just as he had done for Dr Winston Ramsey. He knew that Randal would be frenzied and rabid about the write-up. What he did not know, was that Hadleigh had already been on the receiving end of Randal's intimidation and was only one step away from obliteration.

It all left Hadleigh utterly unprotected and in the inevitable firing line. Carlton was very remiss and unusually oblivious, but Randal's downfall superseded all other possibilities.

The phone rang in Hadleigh's office. It was his private number. His mouth was dry and his heartbeat rapid. He did not want anyone bothering him on his first day back, facing this unbearable plight. He reluctantly answered the call, his hands shaking as he picked up the receiver.

"Hadleigh Masterson here. I'm busy, so please be quick," he almost barked.

"I don't do 'quick'. Not when there are two pages of libel to discuss," replied Randal, with a very intimidating edge to his cultured voice.

Hadleigh nearly gagged. He was petrified.

"Are you receiving me? You see, I'm losing my patience with you, Mr Masterson. In fact, I'm so fucking furious I could spontaneously combust! Just like your intrusive tape recorder and Elvis Ford's camera!"

Hadleigh gasped. Somehow or other he needed to find his voice. He had to explain his innocence, so he cleared his throat repeatedly. His will to survive usurped his fear as he spoke hoarsely.

"Randal... Mr Forbes... you have to believe what I'm going to tell you. I knew absolutely nothing about this dreadful article. I don't even know the journalist. I've been away, you see, and I was stupid enough to leave the editing to my team. Had I read this trashy, offensive report, well, I would have ripped it up and destroyed it for good. I'm so deeply sorry for all the intrusive fallout," he pleaded.

"Intrusive fallout? Is that what you call it? That doesn't come close. It's a character assassination affecting a nationwide unpopularity offensive. I've gone from charming to alarming. From flawless to lawless. From winner to sinner. From fluid to druid. From managing director to Hannibal Lecter. Need I go on? Do you get the poetic drift? Is it all sinking in, Mr Masterson?"

"I don't know w-what to say. It's unforgivable. Please, please, let me retract the whole wretched thing by writing my own column with an emphatic apology. Let me put you on your well-earned pedestal. Furthermore, I'll point my accusatory finger at Fletcher Trent and make everyone aware that *The Announcer* is removing itself from every single syllable in that disgusting article," he pleaded passionately.

"Ah, *removing*! My favourite word! You see, it's far too late for any sycophantic reparation. My name's been dragged through the murky, medieval mud. I'm a paranormal pariah, so I may as well live up to my reputation. What do you say? Should I stretch my lurid legs and go for the journalistic jugular?

Hadleigh gulped. He felt like an unprotected, cornered fox with a pack of hungry hounds baying for its blood. "Please, I'm mortified. You don't deserve this disrespect... this dishonour. It's not my fault. Please believe me. I want to make it right," he begged.

"Do you now?"

"Yes! Yes, I so do!"

"Hmm, well then. Let me see. How can I put this? I don't give a flying fuck about your fawning compensation. I warned you! I couldn't have made it any clearer!" threatened Randal.

"I know you did, but I had no control over any of this! It wasn't of my making!" he implored.

"What kind of a no-mark editor are you? Running away from your prime position and putting second-rate reporters in charge while you tremble in the dark. Praying I wouldn't come after you. Cowardice such as yours deserves first-class castigation! The blame lies at your own dithering door. You, Mr Masterson, are my number-one priority now. How considerate am I? Placing you at the front of a long line of victims. Saving you time queuing up. My charitable attention to detail knows no bounds. I do hope you appreciate my gallantry. You do, don't you?"

Hadleigh began to shake and his lips trembled uncontrollably.

"You still there, or have you deserted your post again?" sniped Randal.

Hadleigh's voice abandoned him in the light of Randal's monstrous threat. What else could he say in order to make him change his mind anyway? Apologies were hopelessly ineffective now. Offers of remuneration had been ruthlessly rejected. The only thing he could expect from Randal was the worst.

"I don't know what else to say to you," whispered Hadleigh.

"Let me help you out on that count. I'll do the talking for you. So, to continue, make the most of it. Whatever you do from this moment will be short-lived. Do you understand me? Now, I have to go and work out a charm offensive that will woo the public back into my charismatic corner. Because of your rag of a paper, I need to employ valuable psychic energy and court the bonehead populace all over again. It's so tiresome when I could be using it solely to remove disaffected blockheads like your simpering self. Tell me, Mr Masterson, were you ever in the boy scouts?"

Hadleigh was petrified but still replied, "Y-yes. W-why?"

"In 1907, Baden-Powell devised the scout's motto. It's applicable. Just two words, Mr Masterson. 'Be prepared'."

Randal slammed the phone down and Hadleigh put his face in his hands. How had this happened? It had been born out of his lifetime's wish for a face-to-face exclusive with his long-time idol. A sought-after dream that had morphed into a deadly nightmare.

He could go to the police for protection, but what would he say? That Randal Forbes was intent on removing him via his telepathic waveband? That it might happen at any time, but he could not pinpoint the actual date? That the article in *The Announcer* was pretty much on the paranormal button and had inflamed Randal's sixth, seventh and eighth senses.

The law won't protect me. It would section me!

Hadleigh had no choice but to sit tight and hope for the impossible. Maybe, just maybe, Randal could still have a change of heart, because regardless of the present impasse, Hadleigh was still going to rewrite, and retract, Fletcher Trent's damning article and place Randal in a virtuous, shining light. Personally, professionally and creatively.

It will take the form of a front-page, grovelling restitution, not only for Randal's reputation but also for my salvation. I've got to try this last throw of the dice and keep hoping for a double six, as opposed to a six-

six-six, satanic combination! With Randal at the forefront of its deadly association!

★★★

Later that same day, Randal visited Clive in his office. He was livid.

"Have you seen this badly written piece of libellous trash?" he asked Clive with an ungodly lustre in his penetrative gaze.

"I was hoping you hadn't," responded Clive in a low voice, his heart pumping ridiculously fast in his chest wall.

Randal ripped out the offending pages as he ranted. "You see, Clive – in order to save you palpitating with nervous anticipation – Hadleigh Masterson has sanctioned his own premature epitaph! So, watch this space!"

★★★

The very same morning that the *Daily Announcer* went to press, with a convincing, apologetic retraction of Fletcher Trent's slanderous report on Randal's lifestyle and reputation, Hadleigh found himself visiting the psychiatric hospital where Elvis Ford had been sectioned. It was long-term because his brain was irreparable, and he needed to be constantly medicated and repressed.

Hadleigh did not really know why he had chosen to go, especially now. Some kind of faceless force had propelled him in that particular direction and nudged him, on a subliminal level, to check on any progress. After all, Elvis had been his freelance photographer and deserved to be called upon.

As he drove to his destination, Hadleigh's vision was far from crystal-clear. It was almost as if he was looking through a light transparent cloth, making everything slightly surreal. He felt strangely spurred on to be with his disturbed cameraman,

153

almost like a journalistic missionary to propagate his human rights.

Back in Weybridge, Randal was pulling every one of Hadleigh's servile strings via the usual vital photographic image. He yawned widely because he was bored rigid with the whole Masterson/Ford saga. It needed putting to bed in order to concentrate on the main man. To focus on his most powerful adversary to date.

Carlton Flint! The Zodiac's own shooting star. But one stellar step at a time.

By rights it should be Fletcher Trent stepping into the literary, landslide limelight. His write-up on Randal was heretical. He needed putting in his poison-penned place as well, but that, too, could wait a little longer.

Today, Hadleigh Masterson was headlining, in a special psychiatric showdown. He was fully under Randal's spell, in a relaxed state, with his mind responding to all external suggestion and forthright commands.

Hadleigh had telephoned the relevant authorities beforehand in order to alert the hospital. As a result, he was expected and would be admitted without question or delay.

"We can't be too careful these days," explained the security officer as he let him inside the door. "Safety is uppermost here, for the patients, staff and visitors."

"Oh, absolutely," agreed Hadleigh.

Once in the corridor, he followed the signs until he approached the ward where Elvis was residing. There were several nurses on duty. The consultant psychiatrist, together with his team, had just finished their rounds. They nodded to him as he passed them and he acknowledged their presence with a smile.

"Who are you visiting, sir?" asked a pretty young nurse with sparkling brown eyes.

"Oh, Elvis. Elvis Ford. He freelanced for my newspaper.

I'm Hadleigh Masterson, the editor of the *Daily Announcer*. He was my photographer, you see."

"Nice to meet you, Mr Masterson. You've just missed his son and daughter. I'm sure they'll be pleased to hear that you've come to see their father, especially in due of their loss and grief."

"Loss and grief?"

"Yes, their mother. She tragically died while visiting Mr Ford in another hospital, before he was admitted here."

"Of course. Of course, I remember now. How very sad. Very sad," he repeated robotically.

He followed her down the ward until he came to the third bed on the right. Elvis was lying on the top, looking at nothing in particular. Hadleigh frowned deeply. Even in his hypnotic state he could see no resemblance to the happy, cheerful man that he once knew. His optimism had been sucked out of him, vacuumed up in some weird, emotional suction, all trace of his innate humour emptied into a humanoid dust bag.

Hadleigh pulled up a chair at the side of his bed and smiled. "Well, hello! Hello there, Elvis. Remember me? I hope you do because I won't forget all the good work you've done for me, and the amazing photographs of A-list celebrities you shot for my newspaper."

Elvis ignored him and just looked vacant.

"You know, I thought I better pay you a visit. This is the first time. Something pulled me here today and now I'm really glad to see you again. Are you pleased to see me?" he asked mechanically.

Elvis blinked then looked to the side. His eyes fastened on Hadleigh's face.

"You do remember me? I'm Hadleigh. So good to see you. Isn't it a nice day?"

Elvis blinked again. His eyes grew wider and his pulse began to race.

"I took a bit of a break recently, but now I'm back in charge.

I don't know why I had an extended holiday. I guess I felt I needed one. I think we all deserve time off, now and then, don't we?"

Randal was in full control and could see Elvis through Hadleigh's eyes. The scene was vivid as he astral-projected himself into the room.

"Would you like to go for a walk? Are you allowed to leave the ward? You must feel really cooped up in here. It's rather warm. Should I ask the nurse? Well, maybe not. I can look after you just as well. It's a lovely day and just the right temperature for you to get some fresh air into your lungs. Do you need a coat or anything before we go out?"

Elvis shook his head. He sat up and swung his legs round to the side of the bed, then put both feet into his navy-blue slippers. He pointed to the door at the end of the ward, as he pulled his dressing gown tightly around him.

"Do you want to go that way with me?"

Elvis nodded.

"OK, then," agreed Hadleigh.

They both walked together: Hadleigh like some mechanism guided by automatic controls and Elvis in the twilight zone fuelled by medication.

They slipped unnoticed through the doorway into a secluded, walled garden with no exit apart from the ward itself. They sat down on a bench which had a plaque dedicated to a former patient who was now intentionally pushing up daisies.

"Have you anything to tell me? Do you still want to take photographs when you get better?" enquired Hadleigh on automatic pilot.

Elvis frowned deeply and two trench-like furrows appeared in the centre of his forehead just above his nose.

"I know that your last camera was badly damaged, but I can buy you a new one if you like? How was it destroyed? I can't remember, Elvis. Can you? Where were we?"

Elvis felt an uncontrollable fury infiltrate his whole being, filling his senses with outrage and violent anger. Randal was in total control of his emotions. For the first time since his induced epileptic fit, Elvis actually spoke. In Randal's voice.

"Hello, Mr Masterson. It's about time you came to see me. You've been on my mind."

Hadleigh twitched. Randal allowed a fraction of recognition to resonate.

"Whose voice is that? I know that voice and it's not yours."

"Bang on the money! Now have a guess."

Randal willed Hadleigh out of his trance, until, bit by bit, he became fully aware of his surroundings and a reality check smacked him hard across his face.

Where the hell am I? Then, as he recognised his companion, Elvis moved in on him with both hands around his throat.

"Now, Mr Masterson, I'm going to wring your scraggy neck, just like your newspaper wrung my career out to dry!"

Hadleigh's eyes bulged out of his head, partly through powerful strangulation but also due to the realisation that Randal was the puppet master pulling all the strings. Elvis was relentless. He squeezed, pressed and throttled until Hadleigh collapsed on the ground, turning blue. Elvis kneeled down and kept up the strangulation to make absolutely sure of his victim's demise. Hadleigh lay sprawled on the path, his bloodshot eyes staring into the distance but seeing nothing.

Randal was satisfied, so he checked out of the Elvis 'Heartbreak Hotel', leaving his destructive baggage behind. There would be no hidden suspicious circumstances surrounding Hadleigh's death. He was being most compassionate, visiting an old friend who was deranged. An open-and-shut case of diminished responsibility resulting in murder. A drug-induced accident waiting to happen. Randal smirked.

Hey ho. Now, on with the rest of the show.

★★★

The Daily Announcer
<u>Tuesday 11th August 1992</u>

Hadleigh Masterson, 29, editor of the *Daily Announcer*, was murdered yesterday by Elvis Ford, a freelance photographer, who was hospitalised with a severe mental health disorder. Strangulation was the cause of death.

We are deeply shocked and saddened by this tragedy, and all our colleagues wish to extend their heartfelt condolences to Hadleigh's family and friends.

A leading psychiatrist where Ford was sectioned gave us the following statement.

"We are very dismayed and utterly regret this tragic occurrence. We knew that Hadleigh Masterson was coming to visit Elvis Ford and we were agreeable.

"We did not consider Ford to be dangerous as he is permanently medicated in order to stop any agitated response or violent reaction. All the time he was a patient here, his condition had been well under control, and we did not think it unfitting for him to have a visitor.

"We are also regretful that not enough attention was paid to his movements. The nurses and doctors were extremely busy and did not notice that both Ford and Masterson had walked out of the side door into the walled garden.

"It should be noted that the area is completely sealed and safe for patients to sit in.

"Apart from this exit, they are totally unable to leave the hospital through any doors or gates. However, a nurse, or family member, usually accompanies patients if they wish to go into the garden. It's not unusual for an inmate to sit on a form there. In Ford's case, we never anticipated a problem with his condition towards anyone in close proximity. He was always

158

subdued and this makes the situation even more tragic for all involved."

Masterson and Ford had worked together several times, the most recent being on an interview with the controversial celebrity Randal Forbes. This tragedy has irony stamped all over it because Masterson, in his capacity as editor of *The Announcer*, had just apologised to Forbes, hot off the press, for the intrusive, defamatory article by Fletcher Trent.

We trust that our comprehensive retraction will make amends for allowing this defamatory article to be featured.

Hadleigh Masterson was a lifelong admirer of Randal Forbes. He was influenced and mesmerised by Forbes' gift for the written word.

We hope that in light of this unforeseen tragedy that all rancour can be put to bed and that Forbes will accept Masterson's posthumous apology in *The Announcer*, on this very sad, poignant day.

A full obituary of Hadleigh Masterson's life and career can be found on Page 5. He will be missed and remembered with great affection and respect.

8

Carlton Flint was blaming himself for Hadleigh's death and questioning why he had overlooked him being the pivotal target, as Randal's next victim. He should have known better and induced another defensive hypnosis, as he had done for all the other helpless casualties.

As he read the various reports on Hadleigh's violent demise, his stomach began to burn as if something was attacking his intestinal tissue. This was the second time in days that he had felt so bad. He swore to himself as the phone rang.

"Francine, phone! Pick it up, please," he grimaced.

"Why can't you answer it? My hands are full of minced fish!" she shouted from the kitchen.

Carlton groaned as he picked up the receiver. "Hello? Can I help you?" he asked, sucking in his breath as a fresh wave of scorching spasm attacked his abdomen.

"Hello, yourself! It's Winston. You sound a bit off. Is everything OK?" enquired the caring physician.

"I guess so, apart from this awful burning sensation in my gut," he moaned.

"Oh? When did that start?"

"A few days ago. Quite honestly, Winston, it's excruciating, but I'm playing it down because I don't want to worry Francine or the girls."

"Do you want me to check you out? It's no bother. I can drive down this Friday because I'm giving another lecture again nearby, so it's no problem at all."

"Would you? It's probably just indigestion. Too much spice, you know." Carlton laughed, but then he winced with another severe contraction.

"I'll see you Friday afternoon then. Probably around four o'clock. Is that OK with you?"

"Whenever. You're always welcome. Why don't you stay with us for the weekend again?"

"That would be delightful, and thanks very much for the invitation. In the meantime, keep off the bloody spice," he admonished.

"I will. See you Friday."

Carlton replaced the receiver. He was more than grateful for Winston's concern. In fact, he had grown very close to him. They shared an unbreakable, unique, loyal bond. A mutual understanding of hidden events.

A secret psychic society.

Francine rinsed her hands under the kitchen taps. She wiped them on a used tea towel, put the towel in the washing machine and then made herself a cup of coffee.

"Carlton, do you want a drink? I've just boiled the kettle," she asked, peeping through the door.

"Yes, please. I'll have a very milky tea. I've got a touch of heartburn, so it'll be soothing." He smiled for her benefit.

"One milky tea coming up then."

She opened the fridge and looked for the bottle. As she scanned the contents a disembodied voice invaded her head. The same one that had entered it twice before. She heard the key word that galvanised her into a state of hypnotic response and action.

Intrusion.

She stood rooted to the spot and moved her head from side to side, like a dog waiting for its owner's next instruction.

Now, Francine. I need you to sprinkle some more corrosive stardust into Carlton's tea. Will you do that for me? For your Scarlet Pimpernel?

"I will," she whispered.

She looked under the kitchen sink and brought out the caustic soda that she normally used as a drain un-blocker, except now it was essential for the command.

Now, lovely lady, put a very tiny amount in the cup and stir it round so it disappears into the hot, milky water. Remember, you've got to destroy Carlton before he kills you. You must defend yourself. Have you done that yet, Francine?

"I have."

Good girl. Now, I want you to invite your best friend Stella to dinner. Make it sound casual. Remember, she's in league with Carlton and wants him for herself after they've killed you. I'm going to help you get rid of them both. Now, when I click my fingers, you'll just carry on as normal. One, two, three, clickety-click.

Francine did all the usual things as if nothing had happened at all. She brought her coffee, and Carlton's spiked tea, into the living room. She kissed his cheek as she gave him his drink and sat down in the opposite chair, crossing her shapely legs.

"Oh! I forgot. Do you want a piece of cake with that?"

"No, it'll only spoil my dinner," replied Carlton, determined to look as normal as possible even though his insides were rebelling.

"Who phoned?" enquired Francine.

"Winston. He's coming down on Friday to give another lecture at the hospital, so I've asked him to stay over again with us for the weekend. Hope you don't mind."

"Not at all. He's the perfect house guest – so caring, polite and kind," she added.

"Indeed."

"Carlton, I've just had a thought. I want to invite Stella for dinner. She's unattached and, come to think of it, so is Winston. I think they should meet each other, and who knows?" she enthused.

"What a good idea. In fact, I don't know why we haven't thought of it before. Give her a ring right now, just in case she gets double-booked."

Carlton thought how lucky he was to have Francine. Her best friend Stella had been through a messy divorce, none of which was her fault. The ex-husband had run off with a much younger woman and she had lost a lot of confidence through the break-up of her marriage. She was extremely attractive and smart. She deserved some good fortune, and Winston could very well be the solution.

Francine rang Stella, who was more than pleased to accept the invitation as she was at a loose end.

"Oh, by the way, there's a doctor friend coming too. He's very charming."

"Are you match-making by any chance?"

"Me? Match-making? Would I do that?" Francine laughed.

"Hmm, see you Friday then, and I'm looking forward to it. Oh, Francine, what's his name?"

"Who?" she teased.

"Don't start. I just wondered, that's all."

"His name's Winston Ramsey and he's a consultant physician. He's the doctor who mostly looked after Carlton when he was in a coma."

"Really?" she responded with more than a touch of interest in her voice.

"See you Friday, Stella."

"See you then. Bye."

Francine was very pleased with herself. *What a good idea I've just conjured up out of nowhere.*

Randal was also patting himself on the back. He had kick-started Carlton's demise. So far, so good. Carlton did not suspect a thing. He telepathically saw Francine in the hallway, so he entered her head again just to make sure that she had totally understood. It was safe to invade, out of Carlton's earshot and vision.

Intrusion.

Francine stood still.

Did you invite Stella for dinner? Remember, you need to kill her as well as Carlton.

"I did. Dr Winston Ramsey will be coming as well," she added.

Randal felt like cart-wheeling all through the house. This could not have gone better if he had planned it himself.

Good! That's more than good! I'm very pleased with you, Francine. Soon you'll be free of Carlton and Stella. But you also need to know this. Winston's a traitor too. He knows all about their plans to murder you and will get some of the insurance money, so he needs to be punished as well. I'll be in touch again and help you.

"I see. Thanks for that. I'm very grateful."

Francine snapped out of her trance at the click of Randal's long, slim fingers. Carlton sipped his tea as she leafed through some magazines. His groaning diverted her attention away from them.

"What's the matter?" she asked with concern, as she saw the pain etched on his face.

"Oh, it's nothing. Just a bit of wind," he lied.

"Well, it doesn't look like that to me. I want you to get it checked out. You can't afford to ignore things, Carlton. You were unconscious for a very long time. I know you're much better now, but just to make sure, go and see the doctor."

"Winston can examine me. That's if I need it. By Friday I'll be fine. It's probably cramp, so don't worry."

Francine frowned as Carlton went to the medicine cupboard to get some painkillers. He swallowed two with tap water, all the time rubbing his torso.

"There, that should do the trick," he reassured, but she was far from convinced.

★★★

Back in Randal-land, he was sat in his study, pen in hand with a large notebook, jotting down ideas for Carlton's abolishment. His imagination was in full flow with ideas pouring out of him, as if he was writing another novel and the character was living in his book.

His trademark cruel smile lingered around the corners of his mouth as he plotted, planned and concocted several variations of the final act. It was just a matter of choosing his favourite ending. Any one of them would suffice, but he always had to skate close to the edge. Just to add that element of risk in order to satisfy his ferocious streak of devilry.

He lit up a cheroot and inhaled his favourite tobacco. He sat back, satisfied with his fertile, imaginative scripts. His barbarity knew no bounds when it was on the verge of another telepathic homicide and only increased in intensity when the well-rehearsed text was actually implemented.

Out of sheer spite, he decided to contact Carlton. He would blank out all his plans, especially Francine's hypnotic subservience. He just needed to add to the drama and taunt Carlton with his latest successful removal. He slid into his head through his photograph. As ever, it was simple but effective.

Here I am again, starman. I know that you pumped Fletcher Trent's thick head full of fanciful ideas about my so-called occultist lifestyle. You must have danced on your starry ceiling when The Announcer *published his ramblings. I bet you had a sunburst moment. Did you laugh your satellite socks off?*

Carlton groaned. Partly due to Randal's unwelcome telepathic communication and also because of the fiery sensation in his alimentary canal.

I'm not in the mood, Randal. I'm so sick and tired of your crazy, lethal games.

We are in a strop! What's the matter, Carlton? Can't stomach the fact that Hadleigh Masterson featured a grovelling apology in his rag of a newspaper to exonerate me from all the libel? A little too late, though, methinks. He's gone to the eternal news desk in the sky. My treat entirely, you understand.

Randal, do us all a favour and disappear up your own egotistical backside. You really are an unfeeling, destructive, perverse piece of work! You're a remorseless and unrepentant assassin. An abomination of a human being!

Thanks for the compliments, Carlton. I wouldn't have expected such accolades from my fiercest rival.

Your reign is coming to an end, Randal. I'm working on it, as I'm sure you're working on mine.

Don't flatter yourself, sunshine. When I annihilate you, it will be off the cuff.

Carlton winced with another wave of pain and Randal had to block out his wicked delight.

Anyway, starman, I'm going to ask you the same question I put to Mr Masterson before I dispensed with his editorial services. Were you ever in the boy scouts?

What's this, Randal, some kind of infantile quiz? Will you go away if I answer?

Without delay.

I was a boy scout. So what?

Two words, Carlton. Be prepared!

Randal pulled out of his brain before he gave too much away. His excitement was peaking and it felt almost orgasmic. He must learn to exercise more control.

After the next homicidal event he could wallow in victorious ecstasy, but until then, he would carry on with his slow-drip, poisonous assault on Carlton's body, administered by the last person on earth that Carlton would suspect: his loyal, lethal spouse, the hypnotised, malleable Francine Flint, armed with deadly sprinkles of corrosive, caustic soda. And that was only the starter. The main course was yet to come.

★★★

Before the ultimate command performance, Randal needed to stretch his daredevil legs. It was a rehearsal prior to the final spark-off between himself and Carlton. His penultimate target would be Fletcher Trent.

He had to rid himself of the sour taste of treasonable tittle-tattle: the collaboration betwixt Carlton and Fletcher that led to the damaging article in *The Announcer* that relegated his esoteric standing. Carlton was the grass, but Fletcher was the journalistic jinx.

So, he has to be punished. And punished he will be.

Randal was sure that Carlton had protected Fletcher against his mental invasion, as he had for Winston Ramsey. So, Randal added yet another versatile bow to his psychic dowry.

His new voice!

A flawless impressionist in full effective flow. A sound that would shatter the hypnotic sanctuary that Carlton had so righteously devised, and render it redundant and ineffective.

If the voice issuing telepathic commands was not Randal's, then the protective spell would be broken and the lethal instruction implemented. It was so simple and could have saved Randal a lot of burning anger at his failed attempt to infiltrate Winston's mindset.

Never mind. That's behind me now and I'm looking forward to the flash-happy future. 'The gift' will shelter me and cast out all imposters and abusers. It will never abandon me, but it will forsake and evacuate all inferior competition that masquerades in its name.

Randal had been busy adding photographs to his file of adversaries. He found the clearest image of Fletcher and placed it right in front of his slate-grey, dazzling gaze. He slid casually inside his head while he observed his whereabouts.

He's in his worn-out car, driving along a country lane on the way to some pointless interview, to perpetuate his journalistic standing in the cut-throat world of 'too many important names with such unimportant minds'.

Randal could see the route through Fletcher's eyes and felt his sweaty, chubby, nicotine-stained fingers on the steering wheel. In the distance he saw a long stretch of road beside a river.

Aha! Here's the ideal opportunity for a quick, no-nonsense completion.

He spoke to Fletcher's mind in the voice of a much older man. Randal's new tone was sonorous, with a slight foreign accent, and was far removed from his own attractive timbre. Fletcher's eyes were already glazed. His driving became erratic as he veered to the left and skimmed the grassy verge alongside the riverbank.

Now, Mr Trent. I'm counting down from ten to one. When I reach number five, steer your rust heap of a vehicle, together with your insufferable ego and poisonous periodicals, to your extreme left. Are you ready for this?

You're the epitome of avarice. You and your fellow intruders, poking your nationwide noses into other people's privacy and pocketing obscene amounts of money for the best harebrained headline. You're all scum!

Randal's startling eyes were glowing with unrestrained malevolence and his senses were alive with merciless retaliation.

OK, here we go. It's such a perfect day for a spontaneous swim. It will cool you down and take the heat out of your swamping schedule. So, listen closely and count down with me. All together now. Ten, nine, eight, seven, six and here comes that proverbial number five. Now, swerve to the left, and keep on driving.

Fletcher obeyed Randal's command without any resistance or contention. The car wheels made contact with the grass verge. He drove without stopping, but his vehicle became immovable, embedded in silted runnels.

Oh, dear! Stuck, are we? Let's see what we can do about that. I know. Get out of your car and just take a little walk to the edge of the river. There's a good little jaded journalist. Keep up the right response and you'll get your reward. The Muppet of the Year badge. A bullshit BAFTA.

Fletcher did exactly what Randal ordered him to do.

So, do take a good, long, hard look at your ugly reflection in the water. I know, I know, it's hard to stomach, but you've lived with it until now.

Fletcher just stared into the river, seeing everything but nothing.

Have you done? Seen enough? Oh, goody. Now, wade into the river and put your head under the water until you feel your tobacco-coated lungs fill up with all the polluted pond life. Because that's exactly what you are. Pond life of the most polluted kind. You know that, don't you? Nod your fat head in agreement, please, and don't stop until I say so.

Fletcher continued nodding until he felt quite unsteady with the constant movement.

A real head-banger. At your own rock concert without the music.

Fletcher's hairpiece fell off and landed in the river.

Whoa! There's a surprise. Stop nodding now and just stand still. You dumpsite dickhead.

Fletcher straightened up and became motionless.

Oh, I am having fun today. I should have filmed this. What can we do now? I still need to be entertained. You can identify with that, can't you? I mean, you keep all your readers amused in your gossip column. That's your form of entertainment. But not for me.

You pulled me to pieces and now I'm going to see you off. I must leave you now because I want you to drown by your own insufferable self. Put your hairless head under the water and stay there. Toodle-pip, Trent, and anchors away!

Randal pulled out of Fletcher's mind the minute his head was submerged. He was delirious with his successful humiliation because he had rid himself of another detractor and, more importantly, he had bypassed Carlton's protective hypnosis for his so-called allies, and all the other defilers of 'the gift'.

★★★

Roxanne was sat in her favourite place: on Randal's knee in his study. She watched him intently as he worked on his text.

"Is this a new book, Daddy?" she asked eagerly.

"Kind of."

"Who's Mr S?"

"Who do you think?" he answered, still scribbling away.

She scanned his head because she did not want to waste any time fathoming it out and it dawned on her pretty quickly. "I know! It's the starman! You're putting him in your story and writing him away! That's what I wanted to do ages ago, but you stopped me! You've gone and pinched my idea." She pouted.

"It's not a story. It's real." He smiled.

"Real? You mean really real? Is it how you're going to kill him? Tell me, tell me now! Let me see!" she squealed.

"Shush, they'll all hear you in the next room! This is just one idea, I've got a few. It's complicated, so be quiet, please," he urged.

Roxanne kissed his face repeatedly. "Can I help? Oh, please let me help!" she pleaded, ignoring his request.

"Maybe, but I don't want you hurt again. I might need you to do your trick of moving things around. There's more than one person I want to hurt, but it's all part of the big plan to finally get rid of the starman for good."

"Why can't I get inside one of the bad people's heads instead? I can, you know. You know I can."

"Because they've probably been hypnotised to ignore your voice, and they won't do what you tell them."

170

"Hypnotised?"

"Yes. The starman made a spell to stop his doctor friend from doing what I wanted him to do."

"How?"

"It doesn't matter. He just did."

"So how will they know what to do?" she puzzled.

Randal's patience was running thin, but she needed to be put in the full picture or she would be asking endless questions. "I can get inside their heads because I've changed my voice and they won't know it's me, so they'll do everything I ask of them now. The starman's wife is already doing what I tell her to do because I hypnotised her and she thinks I'm someone very powerful called the Scarlet Pimpernel."

"I can be another little girl. I can be Little Red Riding Hood or even Alice in Wonderland," she determined.

Randal smiled as he carried on writing. "But it'll still be your own voice, pumpkin. They won't know that you're supposed to be those fairytale children."

"I'll know, and you'll know, though." She poked him with her finger.

Randal put his pen down and held her face in his hands. "But *they* won't know! And that, my little mini-minx, defeats the whole object. Now, will you leave me to work out an ending for the starman and friends? I'll let you know if and when I need your help, but first of all, I have to work out who's doing what to who! Understand?"

"I understand. I'm a good girl, really," she sniffed, tossing back her long red hair in the usual dramatic fashion when she felt slighted at not getting her own way.

Randal laughed out loud at her disgruntled expression.

"It's not funny!" she scolded.

"Oh, but it is; it truly is," he taunted.

"Let me know when you need my help. I'm going to play with Amber now. You know where I am," she replied precociously, as she slid off his knee and walked away in a huff, straightening her violet skirt, which was creased at the hem.

"I sure do, my little purple pocket rocket."

Randal nearly roared with laughter but stopped himself. She would sulk the whole day if he did.

Seven years old, going on eight, going on twenty-one!

Now it's back to the drawing board. So, it's goodbye, Mr Flint, and his tasty but pliable spouse, Francine evergreen. Let's throw in her best friend Cinderella Stella, and last, but by no means least, Winston 'flights-of fancy' Ramsey.

You're all near the finishing line. It's a four-way, slap-in-the-face race. A bricks-and-mortar quarter-final. Who'll qualify first? Now, let me see. What a mammoth murder evening this is going to be! I can't imagine a grimmer dinner. Jack the Ripper, eat your heart out!

Randal shut his large notebook. He would follow his preferred script step by step with perhaps a flourish of improvisation if required. He locked it all away in his desk drawer. On Friday night, he would take it out of its temporary home and bring his words to life. They would dance on the paper in a deadly drama, an epic production. Then, when it was all done and dusted, he would destroy the evidence.

Randal felt aroused.

He looked for Alison because he needed to exorcise the fire running through his red-hot veins. He found her upstairs, changing the bed.

"Don't bother," he instructed with a burning gaze as he glided towards her.

She knew that look only too well. She felt exactly the same inflamed arousal from just one glance. He embraced her, stroking her whole body as he kissed her. He pushed her down onto the bare mattress. His lovemaking was irresistibly intense, but she responded with equal zeal. She always felt obsessed and possessed. That had never altered since the first time in Oxford, all those years ago. It was a madness of almost other-worldly intensity. It would never fade and seemed to get stronger as the years passed by.

She loved him to complete distraction and accommodated him with wild abandon. Randal was lost in the passion of the moment, egged on by his plans for Carlton's demise. It all added to the decadent showmanship, and it was Alison who took the brunt of his lust and passion: willingly, submissively and explosively. He climaxed and cried out with ecstasy, just as Alison peaked and did the same.

Later that afternoon, he ticked off the days on his calendar to the coming Friday. He had been in Francine's head a few times, even instructing her on the menu for her guests. The starter would be a significant dish and he could not wait for the stagecraft to begin.

★★★

The days dragged by until it was the evening of the deadly act. Carlton and Winston were sat in the conservatory chatting, as Francine checked on her chicken casserole and apple crumble. The bell rang and her daughter Maddie went to open the porch door. She smiled through the glass at Stella, who was carrying a bottle of wine and a box of expensive chocolates.

"Hi, nice to see you," said Maddie, as she greeted her mum's best friend.

"You too, you're looking really well. What a fabulous top," replied Stella, admiring Maddie's colourful tunic.

"Oh, thanks. Mum bought it me last week. Zoe's got the same one in green. She's out tonight, so you've just got me for company. By the way, you look gorgeous!"

"Why, thanks, Maddie. I've tried my best," replied Stella, patting herself on the back at such a nice compliment, especially from her best friend's teenage daughter.

She put one side of her thick, blonde hair behind her ear and checked her lipstick in the hall mirror. She did look good in a lilac pencil skirt and jacket, teamed with a violet blouse that matched the colour of her striking eyes.

"Mum's in the kitchen as ever, and Dad's with Dr Ramsey in the garden," explained Maddie.

"Oh, OK," acknowledged Stella casually, trying not to appear too eager to meet Winston.

"I'll tell them you're here."

Stella crossed her fingers behind her back. She was a bit annoyed with herself about her curiosity over Winston and the fact she was hoping for a spark between them both.

Pull yourself together. It's only dinner with friends.

Winston walked with Carlton into the conservatory. He was worried about Carlton's gut ache and wanted him to have a scan.

"I'll have a word with my colleagues down here and get you checked in on Monday," he suggested.

"So, it's just getting through the weekend then," replied Carlton with a grimace.

"I've examined your abdomen. There's no obvious reason for your pain, but we can go to hospital and I'll arrange an X-ray."

"It's not that bad. I'll hang on. It comes and goes."

"Hmm, could be a duodenal ulcer," mused Winston. "Anyway, just say the word if you feel you want it checked out before Monday and I'll come with you."

"I will. Now, let's go. We've got a guest for dinner and I heard the bell ring."

"Guest? Anyone I know?"

"She's Francine's closest friend."

"She? Oh."

Maddie walked in on their conversation to tell them that Stella had arrived and they all headed back to the lounge as Francine came out of the kitchen at the same time.

"Stella! I'm sorry, I didn't know you were here!" exclaimed Francine, as they congregated on the same spot. "Stella, this is Dr Winston Ramsey. Winston, meet my dearest friend Stella Reid."

Winston and Stella were simultaneously impressed as she gave the gifts to Carlton. Winston shook Stella's hand firmly and she responded to his tall, masculine aura. Carlton and Francine looked at each other and smiled.

"Thanks for the wine and chocolates, Stella. Now, anyone for drinks?" asked Carlton.

"Just a white wine for me," replied Winston, still looking into Stella's violet eyes.

"And me," said Stella, still smiling.

They all chatted for a while, each one of them bringing something to the conversation. Francine went to prepare the starter of homemade fish cakes with rocket leaves and asparagus. She began to shape the prepared mixture into thick, round pieces. Halfway into the preparation she stopped dead in her tracks.

Intrusion.

"Hello, Scarlet Pimpernel."

Good evening, Francine. We must get together again soon. But for now, I just want you to ask Stella into the kitchen. Say you need her assistance, but act normally.

"I will."

Francine stood in the kitchen doorway. "Stella? Can I borrow you for a minute, please?" she asked, with a manufactured, casual smile. "Sorry to drag you away, but I need a bit of help here."

"Of course," replied Stella, somewhat reluctant to leave the discussion, especially Winston's attentive company. But she remembered that he was staying for the weekend, so he would not be in any hurry to leave that evening.

Francine was totally under Randal's control.

175

Now, sexy lady, I want you to heat up the oil for your fish cakes and ask Stella to fry them for you. Say you need to see to the main meal, and it would be most kind of her.

Francine did as Randal asked and Stella obliged.

Now, is the oil really hot? Don't speak, just nod your head.

Francine nodded.

Grab Stella's hands tightly and force them into the frying pan. Hold them down by her wrists so she can't pull away.

Francine looked like a mesmerised Stepford wife on a programmed mission. She seized Stella's hands and immersed them into the bubbling, flammable liquid. Stella screamed so loudly that it reached the ears of the next-door neighbours, even though the Flints' house was detached and in its own grounds.

"What the hell are you doing! Let go of me!" she screeched.

Randal pulled out of Francine's head.

"Oh my God!" shrieked Francine. "Stella! What have you done?"

"What have *I* done? *You* did it!" she cried.

"What's going on here?" asked Carlton, as they all came rushing into the kitchen.

"Stella's burned her hands badly in the hot oil," squealed Francine.

"This isn't good. She needs immediate treatment," advised Winston, as he examined the burns. "I'm driving you to the hospital right now."

Stella was in too much pain for explanations. She felt sick.

Winston put his arm around her shoulders and comforted her as best he could. They made their way over to his car, which was parked in the double garage.

"Listen, everyone, I'll see to Stella. You needn't come with. I'll keep in touch and let you know what's happening," he said, taking complete charge.

"Where's your mother?" Carlton asked Maddie, when Francine seemed to have disappeared.

176

"She was in the kitchen. She must be emptying the oil or something," replied Maddie, who was visibly upset.

Carlton frowned. Something was not quite right. He looked for her, but she was not there. The offending pan was still on the switched-off gas ring. A drawer had been left wide open. The meat cleaver was missing.

Winston helped a sobbing Stella into the passenger seat of her car. She was crying and her badly burned hands needed swift attention. He was just about to get into the driver's seat when Francine appeared behind him, brandishing the misplaced cleaver. She swung it high above him and then brought it down on his skull, slaughtering him instantly. The sight was horrific as he fell forwards into the car, with his butchered head touching Stella's right leg. Francine looked possessed as she snarled at Stella.

"So! You think you can take my husband away from me? Do you? Do you? Bitch! You and Carlton, plotting to kill me, and getting the insurance money after I die? All of you conspiring against me! I've killed Winston because he's in on it, and now I'm coming for you!" she growled in a deranged voice.

Stella passed out with the shock. Then the axe moved out of Francine's grip on its own and journeyed through the air. It travelled around the car to where Stella had fainted and then, with one swoop, killed her outright. A flow of blood was spreading like a spilt can of red paint, all over the car seats and garage floor.

Randal snapped his fingers and brought Francine out of her trance. Roxanne hugged him for letting her have a part in the homicidal play. It was her who made the cleaver do its second job on Stella, and she was well pleased with the end result.

Carlton walked in on the scene. His jaw dropped open as he absorbed the horrific sight before him. Francine was covered in blood and the cleaver was lying near Winston and Stella's trashed heads. She screamed and could not stop when she saw the carnage. Her eyes were giant saucers of terror as she looked down and saw the splodged red stains on the front of her pretty lemon dress.

"Oh my God! What's going on? Carlton, what have I done? I can't remember! Oh, please help me! I can't remember!" she cried repeatedly.

Carlton felt a burning attack in his volcanic gut. He doubled up and dropped to his knees with the excruciating pain.

"What's wrong, Carlton? Oh God, what's happening here?" sobbed Francine.

Intrusion.

Francine stopped crying instantly as Randal induced a hypnotic trance. She stood still, waiting for her next command, and Randal entered Carlton's head to gloat.

Hello, starman. Having a nice get-together? We're having a jolly old time at this end. Francine has been the perfect hostess for my evening's entertainment. She's very compliant, don't you think?

Carlton was in agony from the caustic soda that Francine had spooned into his last drink. He was beside himself with pain and hatred.

You fucking monster! You insane psychopath! I'm going to kill you! You piece of satanic shit!

Dearie me, the righteous one in cursing mode! Not very angelic now, are we? It's amazing how your language is corrupted when you've been usurped by your closest enemy. Now you know how I felt each time you elevated the upmanship.

Carlton was furious with himself. How could he have overlooked Francine's possession? He ought to have realised that her actions were out of character. He should have seen the hypnotic signs or had a psychic notion that all was not right.

Don't beat yourself up, starman. Your wife's the perfect go-between, so warm, soft and sexy. Easy to manipulate. In fact, she was repeatedly up for it when we met at a hotel recently. Quite insatiable.

You unspeakable, psychopathic maniac! You used my wife to cause the carnage tonight! To lure her dear friend, and mine, to their deaths? You bastard!

Don't forget the caustic soda, Carlton. That was a classy touch.

I'm going to murder you! I'm ready for you now!

And I'm more than ready for you, starman! So, bring it on!

Carlton's eyes began to radiate with ultra-violet, bright-blue beams of intense light as he entered Randal's psychic arena. His wrath was so fierce that Randal felt his head jerk violently backwards with the surge. For a moment he could not breathe and Roxanne felt his struggle.

"Get away! Get out of the room now!" Randal pleaded with her.

"No! No, Daddy! You need me here!" she cried.

Carlton stepped up on his assault. He wanted to kill Randal stone dead. His philanthropic benefaction had flown out of the well-meaning window. The pain in his gut increased, but so did his fury. In fact, it was enhancing his appetite for revenge.

Randal's eyes laser-beamed across the room, like floodlights on a dark background, slicing through the semi-twilight setting. The battle scorched on and on. Randal's brain felt so violated he nearly blacked out. Carlton was winning the telepathic war.

"Daddy! Oh, my Daddy!" cried Roxanne, as he fell to the floor holding his head.

"Get out! Get out now!" he urged, but she would not leave him.

Francine was still hovering under Randal's hypnotic spell, but it was wearing off slowly with his weakened state. He would just have to take a chance on her remaining mesmerised.

He dug deeply into his cabbalistic reserves and fought back. He conjured up a vehemence of heroic symmetry, matching Carlton brain to brain, mind to mind and force to force. Now it was Carlton's turn to flag. The burning sensation in his stomach created a weak moment of distraction and its scorching let Randal completely back into the race.

Randal stood up and pumped his lethal, combative injection of pure psychic poison into Carlton's declining form. Roxanne held his hand as she re-entered the fiendish fray and spoke to Randal's mind.

Daddy, let me help! I know what to do! Please, please, please!

I don't want you here! Stay away! Do as I say, it's too dangerous!

But I know what to do! I know what to do!

She ignored his request. She looked at Francine's photograph and entered her head so she could see through her eyes. She focused on the blood-stained cleaver lying on the floor, while the encounter of two equally powerful psychics carried on. Randal's resolve was relentless. Carlton's determination was resolute.

Roxanne's eyes glowed as she focused on the cleaver. Her stare was incandescent and remorseless. The axe shifted and then moved in mid-air.

Randal raped Carlton's senses. Carlton assaulted Randal's brain. It was a terrifying tit-for-tat impure incursion, spurred on by mutual hatred and detestation. The loathing and rancour permeated every thought and sensation in both of their heads.

Roxanne willed the meat cleaver in Carlton's direction. It flew through the air towards her intended target. Her eyes became two pin-points of lethal ignition as she guided the object on its way to the desired aim.

Randal was flagging again. Even though Carlton was violated, his absolute abhorrence of Randal's whole essence spurred him on to another level of attack. Randal struggled to breathe and his lungs almost caved in. He was beginning to regret the taunting which had kick-started this final conflict. But on the other hand, there could only ever be one victor.

Carlton's venom was pumping its deadly flow into Randal's body and he collapsed on the floor. Randal felt telepathically thrashed, as he rolled over from side to side in agony. Carlton was relentless and completely invaded Randal's senses.

I'm going to kill you! The world will be a better place! Die! Die! Die!

Randal was beaten. He truly felt his mortality. He knew he was close to death as his whole life flashed before him. His radiating eyes were bulging out of his head as his entire body felt violated. Carlton sent him flying across the room. He hit the wall. His ribs cracked and he yelled out in pain.

Then, suddenly, and unexpectedly, Carlton pulled away. Randal felt him abruptly vacate his brain: a complete and thorough withdrawal. He scanned the scene through his all-seeing, scorched eyes.

Carlton slumped forward and then lay face down on the garage floor. Buried in between both shoulder blades sat the versatile meat cleaver that had caused the multiple murders at the doomed dinner party.

Randal was panting and sweating profusely, his breathing totally jeopardised. Roxanne cried as he looked up at her tiny, appealing form.

"Don't shout at me, Daddy, but I had to kill the starman. He hurt me bad and I had to do it because he was hurting you bad too. I'm a good girl, really."

Randal could not answer. He was still struggling to breathe.

"I just wanted him dead and not hurting you anymore. I hate him. You would have beat the starman in the end, Daddy. I know you would have, but I wanted him gone with the axe."

Randal crumbled. He was physically and mentally exhausted.

"Daddy! Oh no! I've got to make you right!"

Roxanne kneeled down and lay beside him, listening to his shallow breathing. She found a handkerchief in his trouser pocket and used it to wipe away the sweat running down his face, as she spoke out loud to him. "I know Uncle Clive does this for you, too. But I'll look after you this time. I know how to make you good," she said, kissing his hot cheek.

Randal needed to let her know that he would eventually recover on his own and found the strength to speak. "No… pumpkin. It's… it's… too much… for you. I just… need… time to… come round. You're… too… little… to use… so… much… power."

Roxanne completely ignored his advice.

She put her tiny hands around his ribs. They grew hot and radiated with healing vibrations that journeyed to the very source of his depletion. She moaned as she felt his damaged consciousness and stepped up her soothing psychic remedy.

After a while she laid her head on his chest, which was convulsing with defective respiration. The heat travelled through him, repairing and restoring everywhere it flowed.

"No… more. I'm… feeling… better," rasped Randal, as his body readjusted to a bearable normality.

Roxanne had fallen asleep on him. He sat up, holding her in his arms. She was spark out but safe. He would recharge her battery cells, but for now, she needed to sleep. Then after a while, he would revive her completely.

My precious little purple pocket rocket. Your daddy loves you more than life itself. The starman gave me a marathon run for my money. I really hope he's dead and not just injured.

I fought back, but the winning prize was up for grabs and it would have gone his way. Sleep, my baby girl. Your daddy will take care of you now and never let anyone harm you again.

I gave you life, and you undoubtedly saved mine.

'The gift' will live on. But only through us.

9

Three police cars and two ambulances surrounded Carlton's house. His daughter Maddie had called them in hysterics and now she was in a state of absolute shock. She had previously found her mother in the garage doorway, screaming and covered in blood. Inside were the dead bodies of Winston and Stella, with both of their heads severely wrecked. Her father lay face down on the garage floor with a meat cleaver wedged in his back.

Every neighbour in the affluent vicinity had come out of their homes and congregated in the tree-lined road. They watched as the police took Francine away, handcuffed, blooded and unhinged.

"I didn't do it! I didn't do it! It wasn't me! It was the Scarlet Pimpernel! He made me! I don't know why! I don't know why!"

Randal had recovered enough to re-enter her head and influence her speech. He stroked Roxanne's hair back off her damp forehead as he observed the scene through Francine's wild eyes. He zoomed in on Carlton's body as the ambulance men carried him, face down, on a stretcher. The axe was still immersed in his back as Randal heard their conversation.

"He's still alive. It's critical, but there's a pulse."

No! I can't let him live! He knows too much! I've got to work this one out. I can still get inside his brain. It shouldn't be too hard. I've got absolute power over him in this state. There's no Dr Winston Ramsey anymore to pull him through. I'm the puppet master.

Starman, I'll finish you off! Your killer wife will be straight-jacketed for life and your daughters will be damaged and ostracised, and nobody, I repeat nobody, will want to be associated with the name of Carlton Flint or any of your fucked-up family.

Randal carried Roxanne upstairs to bed. She was still sleeping soundly. He sat on the edge of the mattress and stroked more damp red curls away from her beautiful face. He sighed deeply. How was he going to tell her that Carlton was still breathing the same air?

Moving a meat cleaver with her mind, in order to achieve a double killing, was astonishing. She was still a child, his special offspring, but a fledgling. Her tenacity would not let her leave him alone in the battle for psychic supremacy. She had defied his every request for her to vacate the room, to move far away from Carlton's rage. She had put Randal's safety before her own: selflessly, loyally and imposingly. His love for her was overflowing, not measured in human terms alone.

Downstairs, Alison was puzzled where they both were. "Ryan, have you seen your dad or Roxanne? Did they go for a walk together or something?"

"I think they were in his study before. I've been busy on my computer," he said distractedly.

"Amber, sweetie. Have you seen them?"

"I saw Daddy carrying Roxanne upstairs," she answered, engrossed in her favourite television programme.

"Carrying her? Why? Is she OK?"

Amber just shrugged. Alison frowned and then climbed the stairs. Roxanne's bedroom door was slightly ajar. She opened it to find Randal sat on the edge of the bed, stroking her damp, flushed cheek in a loving gesture.

"Randal, what's wrong? She's not ill, is she?"

"She's just very tired. I don't think she slept well last night. Another nightmare with Saul and Maxine in it," he lied.

"Oh, poor chicken. It's so unfair to lose both parents the way she did, and so very young. It's bound to affect her. I feel for her so much. I've truly grown to love her like my own."

"Me too," whispered Randal, and held out his hand to Alison.

She sat next to him and he put a protective arm around her shoulder.

"You know, Roxanne thinks of you as her real mother now. She told me so. You're doing such a great job with her. You're so good, making her feel loved and part of the family," he said with misty eyes.

"It's a labour of love, but let me tell you that she adores you more than anyone. She would follow you to the moon and back. I don't blame her. We all would."

Randal smiled. His love for Alison was infinite, but he would on no account reveal his or Roxanne's psychic standing to her. It would have to be their eternal secret. Alison would never understand 'the gift' and all the responsibility that was required to maintain its majesty. Her mortal response to their telepathic removals would be one of abhorrence, shock and disbelief. She would want to vacate his life and leave a massive hole in his soul.

If she ever found out he would need to hypnotise her away from it all, but he would still be on edge over her discovery. She could never be party to that piece of him, or to Roxanne's inheritance. Only Clive was privy to their hidden cause. He had the complex honour and complicated management, as their loyal protector.

Even Clive relapsed with it all. He's going to totally freak out over this latest production. I've got to prepare him for the gruesome details. In fact, I'm going to phone him right now.

"I promised Clive I'd ring him over some business that's cropped up. You coming down?" he asked Alison.

"Soon. I just want to make sure that Roxanne's OK. I'll sit here with her in case she wakes up or has another nightmare."

Randal nodded. It was safer to let her believe in that distorted theory. He blew her a kiss as he left the room and went back down to his study. Ryan and Amber were having a disagreement over a TV programme, so everyone was occupied. He opened the door to his death-dealing den, poured himself a large glass of bourbon and lit up a cheroot.

He had one more telepathic glance through Francine's eyes at the finale of the night's lethal entertainment. He needed to be kept up to date with the latest developments. Francine was being interviewed in a stark room at the police station. She was still overwrought and in a state of severe confusion.

"I can't remember! I can't remember anything! I would never, never, never hurt my husband or my closest friend. I'm heartbroken, please believe me," she sobbed, and the tears cascaded down her cheeks. Her mascara was badly smudged, making her look like a certifiable panda.

"Who's the Scarlet Pimpernel?" asked Detective Inspector Wayne Bredbury.

"Who? What are you talking about?"

"When we arrested you at your house, you said that the Scarlet Pimpernel made you do it. Do what, Mrs Flint?"

"I don't remember. I'm… I'm so confused."

"You're covered in blood, Mrs Flint. The blood of your victims. What had they done to make you kill them?"

"I didn't kill anyone! Why would I?" she screamed.

"You tell me. Why would you?"

"I don't know! I can't remember!"

Francine put her head in her hands and sobbed uncontrollably. Randal seized the moment to justify her guilt.

Intrusion.

She stopped crying instantly and sat upright in her chair.

"Yes, Scarlet Pimpernel," she replied readily and calmly.

Repeat after me the following, word for word.

"I will."

Detective Inspector Bredbury listened to her regulated voice and saw the trance-like expression on her face. He noted that she had gone from hysteria to composure in the space of a few seconds.

Francine spoke Randal's words out loud. "I had to kill them all. My husband, Dr Winston Ramsey and Stella Reid. Carlton and Stella were having an affair and were planning to kill me, then cash in a life insurance policy after my death. Dr Ramsey knew about it and was in on it as well. I had to kill them with the meat cleaver before they murdered me. I'm totally guilty and I would do it all again in a heartbeat."

After she had duplicated Randal's words, she kept turning her head from side to side like a dummy waiting for its ventriloquist to bring it to life.

Detective Inspector Bredbury cleared his throat and spoke. "Francine Flint, you have just admitted, and I have recorded your confession, that it was yourself who murdered Dr Winston Ramsey, Stella Reid and also critically injured your husband, Carlton Flint, with the intention to kill him outright using a meat cleaver. Francine Flint, I am arresting you for the murder of the two deceased, and the intended murder of your husband, Carlton Flint. You do not have to say anything, but it may harm your defence if you do not mention when questioned something which you later rely on in court. Anything you do say may be given in evidence."

Randal spoke to her mind and she echoed his words again. "There's someone else who helped me. You were right. It was the Scarlet Pimpernel who told me what to do. He made me put caustic soda into my husband's drinks so he would be in permanent pain before I killed him. He deserved it."

"I see," replied Detective Bredbury. He looked at his sergeant.

"She's insane. Psychotic, schizoid or both," said his colleague.

187

"Take her down to the cells. Handcuff her again and I'll arrange a psychiatric assessment. I'm going to speak to someone now. I don't want her topping herself before the morning," he instructed.

Randal pulled away and Francine fell back down to earth with a frenzied bump. The trauma of her plight hit her and she began to cry again with great convulsive sobs. Randal inhaled his cheroot smoke and left her alone to stew.

Enough of that drama. Now I've got to tell Clive what to expect. Forewarned is forearmed.

He rang Clive and inhaled deeply as he waited for him to answer. He blew out the smoke and watched it curl around the room.

"Hello. Clive Hargreaves, can I help you?"

"Hi, it's me."

"Hi, what can I do for you?" asked Clive suggestively, his heart skipping its forever usual beat at the sound of Randal's voice.

"Are you sat down?"

"Why? Should I be?" replied Clive, as a slither of apprehension travelled along the length of his spine.

"Take a seat. I've got something to tell you. You need to know what's happened this evening."

Clive felt his legs go weak. What kind of evil scenario had transpired for Randal to call him up in this manner?

"Go on. I'm sat on a chair and I'm all ears."

"It's not pretty, but it was very necessary."

"It's always anything but pretty, and not necessarily necessary," gulped Clive.

"In this case, that's highly debatable. It concerns the loathsome Carlton Flint and his deluded spouse. Flint's been taunting me and spoiling for a telepathic fight. I've never forgiven him for hurting Roxanne, for sending her flying through the air and banging her head against the wall. Neither has she."

"Flying through the air! Banging her head on the wall! You let her join you in some psychic revenge ritual?" admonished Clive.

"I was wrong, but that's done and dusted now. It's this evening's performance I need to fully explain to you. It's epic."

"I need a cigarette. And a drink! Wait there," groaned Clive, dreading what Randal was going to say.

Clive's hands trembled as he lit up and knocked back a shot of whiskey. "OK, shoot. Shoot before I chicken out altogether," he instructed hoarsely.

"Don't interrupt me; just let me talk. The hatred I have for Carlton Flint goes beyond any loathing I've ever had before. I hypnotised his wife to obey me. I told her to sprinkle caustic soda into his drinks to cause abdominal pain. I needed him to be in a weakened state. I made her believe that Carlton wanted to kill her in order to collect the money on her life policy, and that he was having an affair with her best friend Stella Reid. Also, that Dr Winston Ramsey was in on the act, Carlton's ally and saviour who knew everything about me and 'the gift' thanks to Flint's loose tongue."

Clive began to shake in anticipation of a horrific scenario.

"Do you want me to carry on? I can feel your fear," verified Randal.

"I need to know," croaked Clive.

"To continue, Francine threw a dinner party this evening and they were all there. I told her to ask Stella to fry some fish cakes. I made her hold Stella's hands in the hot oil, causing severe burns. Dr Ramsey saw that she needed urgent medical attention, so he helped her into his car in order to drive her to the hospital. I instructed Francine to pick up the meat cleaver in the kitchen drawer. She followed them into the garage and killed Ramsey with the axe. I made her accuse Stella of wanting her dead so she could collect the insurance money and run off with Carlton. Then Roxanne stared at the—"

"*Stop!* Stop right there! Roxanne was with you when all this was going on! She put herself in danger so you could perform your deadly script? Randal, what the hell were you thinking of?

How could you put her at risk! *Again!*"

"Let me finish! You need to understand why. I tried repeatedly to get her to leave the room, but she wouldn't and didn't. It was just as well, otherwise I wouldn't be talking to you now. The part she played saved my life.

"She saved your life! Oh my God! What happened, Randal? What went on? I can't bear it!" wailed Clive.

"Calm down. I don't want you relapsing again. Please, Clive, it's all under control now. I'm telling you this because it will reach the ears and eyes of the intrusive media, and it's best you hear it all from me, first-hand."

"Go on then," replied Clive, breathing heavily.

"Are you calm?"

"Are you kidding?"

"Clive, you have to know what's happened, but if you want me to stop, then I will," confirmed Randal.

"No, carry on, I need to know."

"OK. As I was saying before you freaked out, Roxanne focused on the axe in Francine's hand. She caused it to move away, on its own, around the car and then kill Stella. Carlton came looking for her in the garage and saw the carnage. Then it was just him and me in a telepathic showdown. It was rampant: unbelievably savage and intense. I was overcome, then victorious, then overcome again. I was on the verge of total collapse when Roxanne telepathically moved the cleaver in Carlton's direction and it lodged in between his shoulder blades. He withdrew and fell face down on the floor. Without her intervention, I would have died. Such was the intensity of Flint's rancour and wrath."

Clive could not reply. He went into full panic-attack mode. His breathing was very audible.

"Clive, listen to me. It's all OK. Roxanne's sleeping but safe and I'm fit enough to be talking to you about it. It's under control."

Clive found his voice. "Under control? You call that under control? I nearly lost you and three other people are dead," he gasped.

"Two. Flint's still alive."

"Alive? With a hatchet buried in his back! Is he Superman or something?" asked Clive disbelievingly.

"His mortality is under threat. If he dies from his injury then that's the perfect ending. If he doesn't then I'll have to make sure that he does."

"Oh, God. What about his wife? What's happened to her?"

"She's banged up, off her trolley and blaming the Scarlet Pimpernel."

"The Scarlet Pimpernel? What!"

"That's who she thinks I am. I hypnotised her to believe it. She'll go down for murder with diminished responsibility and be sectioned. That's about it," concluded Randal.

"That's about it! That's about it! Oh, well, that makes everything hunky dory then, doesn't it? It doesn't matter a jot that her two daughters have got to live with the fact that their mother will be wrongly accused of killing two people, soon to be three, when you effect Carlton's death! A much-loved husband and father! Their lives will be decimated!"

"Would you rather it was me lying on the concrete floor stone dead? Because I swear to you, Clive, I was only a whisker away from extinction."

Clive shuddered, his whole body a mass of nervous tension. "I warned you, Randal. Didn't I warn you that one day something could go drastically wrong and we all could lose you? If that happened, I wouldn't want to live."

"It's not going to happen."

"Without Roxanne's help it would have! She stepped into your paranormal playground. How could you let her do that? Carlton would have left you alone. He was no threat at all until you goaded him."

"He had to be brought down. Imposters or enemies of 'the gift' will always need to be removed," replied Randal resolutely.

"And another thing," accused Clive, "how come you're talking normally after such a mental violation? You're usually spark out, even in victory."

"Roxanne again. She healed me."

"Roxanne! Nearly eight years old and taking on this heavy responsibility, creating two bloodthirsty murders and saving your life into the bargain! Where's the poetic justice in that? In human terms she's just a kid. Just a kid," he repeated in a tense voice, close to tears.

"You think I don't know that! I didn't want her involved, but she insisted. She dug her little heels in and ignored my advice, my orders and even my status. She defied me in every way. In the end it was just as well or I wouldn't be talking to you now."

"While you're in confessional mode, who else have you removed this year? I want the truth, Randal. There's been a spate of deaths, all your connections. Be honest with me for once!" beseeched Clive.

"You really want to know?"

"No, but I really *need* to know. As your protector."

Randal sighed deeply. He was so tired of justifying his removals, but Clive was only going to pump him repeatedly if he hid the names.

"In assassination order then, for your ears only. Reggie Sommers, Gemma Ford, Hadleigh Masterson and Fletcher Trent," replied Randal, omitting Spencer because that would be too near the knuckle and would affect Clive badly.

"I see."

"Anything else?"

"Why? Is there more? Is there something in the ominous offing? Another victim trembling in their bed at night, waiting for you to obliterate them?"

"Nothing urgent. Apart from Flint," responded Randal cruelly.

"Of course! I mean he's a must for the funereal list! Dear God, I should really hate you, Randal."

"And do you?"

"You know damn well I don't. I could never hate you. I just hate the inhuman things you do."

Randal said nothing and the sound of silence was deafening to Clive's ears.

"I'll never understand, but you must have your own reasons for removing them."

"I always do, Clive."

"Yes. You always do."

"Have I your permission to go now? Are you OK about it all, or do you need to talk it out some more?" asked Randal.

"It's done. You can't undo it. I'll have to live with it. As ever."

"Please do. Don't ever go. I need you, Clive, and so does Roxanne. Always."

"I know. I'll see you tomorrow."

"Remember now, the news will be full of it. Flint's a huge celebrity and the headlines will be screaming at you. Don't read or listen to any of the reports. It will just make you ill. Promise me?"

"I promise, Scarlet Pimpernel."

A smile played around the corners of Randal's mouth at Clive's cryptic reference to his pseudonym. "Now that's the ticket! I do love you, you know," and with that last endearment, Randal put down the phone.

Clive was utterly aghast at Randal's exploits. It was not the first time, and it would not be the last instance he would find himself in such turmoil. His thoughts were racing round and round, like a sports car on a cylindrical track.

He would never accept Randal's insatiable thirst for homicidal revenge. It was totally abhorrent and a million miles away from the life Clive would have chosen for himself. But the thought of never seeing Randal again was far, far worse than any of his crimes. Clive bit his lip.

God, help me. I adore him. I always have and I always will. And now there's Roxanne as well. She's a living, breathing part of him, so how could I not adore her? But, why, oh why, does he have to persist with this never-ending killing spree? I'm afraid he's quite insane. Psychotic, dangerous and deranged.

But I'll never get tired of looking at him, of being with him. His physical beauty is breath-taking. His touch, his tenderness, his love. His creative genius is unstoppable. I'd die for him. Like Roxanne would. Except she's got her whole life ahead of her. And she needs special attention. And that's my role. That will always be my role.

I know he truly cares for me. His eyes tell me so. Those alien eyes that cause so much pain and death. And yet he saved my life when I was dying. God forgive me and provide me with the strength to carry on. I have to. I love him so. I love him so.

★★★

"I can't believe this! I just can't take it all in," gasped Alison, covering her face with her hands and peeping through her splayed fingers at the television news coverage of the ill-fated, brutal evening.

Randal shook his head in false disbelief, but mentally he was already working on Carlton's demise.

"Francine seemed so friendly and welcoming when we went there for dinner. They were the perfect couple. Their daughters must be devastated. I feel so sorry for them. It's unreal," she concluded.

"You never know what goes on behind closed doors, Alison."

Especially ours! Oh, if only you knew, my cherished wife, but my lips are forever sealed.

"Have you heard from Dean? Did he keep in touch with Carlton, you know, after all the hoo-ha at Astral TV?"

"No. I've heard nothing, and quite honestly, I don't know if he stayed friendly with the Flints. He didn't tell me."

Randal was feeling irritated with all the fuss in the media and Alison's additional questions.

"Do you think that Carlton will pull through again? He astounded the doctors when that awful screen fell on his head. He was a real fighter. We all thought he would never wake up."

I wish he would have kicked the blackout bucket there and then! All this commotion could have been avoided! He just won't expire!

"Randal, you're ignoring me! I asked you if you think that Carlton will pull through again?"

"How should I know? I'm not a clairvoyant!"

"Why are you so offhand with me?" she protested. "This is a triple tragedy and we know two of the people involved. Not to mention their daughters!"

Randal toned down his short-tempered touchiness. "I'm sorry. Look, I know it's bad, but what can we do about it? Francine Flint is obviously loco and now she's awaiting justice. Their doctor friend is no more, her close pal has snuffed it and her husband's fighting for every breath he takes. As disastrous as it all is, we should not get emotionally, or personally, involved. Selfishly speaking, I've had enough press intrusion to last a lifetime. Trial by media has been my middle three names! So as grievous as this all appears to be, quite frankly, we should keep our distance. We've got three children of our own to protect, and we must keep them well away from snap-happy pressmen and TV camera crews."

"I know you're right, but I still can't help feeling pity for their daughters. It's just my maternal side wanting to comfort them," she sighed.

"Comfort them in your heart, but please, Alison, don't get too close to the situation," preached Randal.

Alison sighed again and then switched off the television.

"Hey, Mum! I was watching that!" complained Ryan.

"Well, watch something else, please. Your dad's right. There's nothing any of us can do. Change the subject or the channel."

195

Roxanne was sat with Amber at the table playing snakes and ladders, or at least pretending to be, but inside she was furious. She spoke to Randal telepathically as she threw the dice for her next move.

I'm so, so, so mad! That's the second time I've tried to kill the starman and messed up. Why won't he die?

Oh, he will, my little pocket rocket. Believe me. He will.

She looked up at him and their alien eyes met in a glance of mutual understanding and empathy.

"I won! Beat you!" boasted Amber, as she climbed the ladder to the winning square.

"Well done," replied Roxanne sportingly, but she could not give a fig about it.

The only defeat that was affecting her badly was her failure to kick Carlton's bucket by proxy. All she wanted was a no-nonsense, straight-forward, fatal assignment, with the desired result. So far, Carlton had rubber-balled himself out of terminal injury.

Not this time. My daddy will make sure of that. He can now, because the starman's weak.

Randal read her thoughts.

Don't you worry, pumpkin. I'm going to blast the starman into outer space. He'll never get back to Planet Earth.

Really, Daddy? You're sending him away in a spaceship? Like ET?

I'm just using fancy words. What I mean is I'm going to finish him off for good so that he never bothers us again.

Please do it soon.

Trust in your daddy. This time he won't recover. I'll make sure of it. He'll be as dead as a dodo.

What's a dodo?

It's a one-time bird that couldn't fly.

A bird that couldn't fly?

It doesn't matter. All that matters is that the starman will be as dead as one.

Promise?

Promise.

I love you, Daddy.

Of course, you do. I love you too.

Randal smiled his special smile at her and her heart sang. What a lovely day it was turning out to be after all. She had Randal's love and a promise to kill the starman soon. What more could she want? She was positively glowing with the anticipation.

The phone rang and Ryan answered it. It was Dean.

"Dad, it's Dean, and he wants to speak to you."

Randal moaned inwardly. *Another shocked family member wanting to discuss the Flints.*

"Hi, I presume you're calling about the murders," predicted Randal.

"Have you ever seen anything like it? My God! Who'd have thought that she was such a basket case? She seemed so normal. I can't get my head round it. And as for Carlton, even if he makes it, how's he going to live with the fact that his own wife wants to kill him?"

"He might not make it. Maybe it would be better if he didn't," responded Randal in a philosophical tone.

"That's really cruel, Rand. I mean his daughters wouldn't want to be deprived of their father as well. They've already lost their mother to some weird psychosis, and they'd have to go through life knowing she's a triple killer."

"Look, Dean. I'll say the same to you as I've said to Alison. We can't get involved in this. I know it's tragic, but there's absolutely nothing any of us can do to change the situation. It is what it is."

"But I felt really close to Carlton when I worked with him on *Celestial Bodies*. We had a great relationship and he became more of a friend. It's only charitable to see if there's anything I can do to help him. Surely you can understand that?"

Randal felt like slamming down the receiver. "If you feel

that way, well, that's your decision. I don't wish to sound heartless, but I'm indifferent to it all. I've had a belly-full of media intrusion this year, and I need to step out of the spotlight for a while. If I get involved with this case, the press will be crawling all over my family again. Alison and the kids were really upset by it last time and I don't need an action replay. You were much closer to Carlton, so do what you think is right," he advised, but mulled it over inwardly.

Carlton's card is marked, Dean. You won't have time to help him because he'll be dead before midnight. Now, Flint-off and leave me to what I do best. Extermination!

***

Randal went back into his study and, without delay, entered Carlton's head, below the threshold of sensation. He was awake but drowsy, pumped full of antibiotics and painkillers. Randal heard the doctor discussing his case.

"We're very pleased with you, Mr Flint. The cleaver was removed to avoid infection and spinal-leak fluid. You were fortunate, if that's the right word. The blade passed through what we call the inter-laminar space, via the mid-portion of your spinal cord and into the vertebral body. Amazingly there was no evidence of significant vascular injury. The area around has been irrigated and cleaned with iodine solution and closed with suture. Your neurological function, immediately after removal of the cleaver, remained the same as before. It really is quite remarkable that you've survived intact. Your daughters have just left but are returning soon. They are so relieved."

Carlton felt a slight sensation in his head but was far too concerned about Francine to even realise it was Randal in residence.

"What's happened to my wife?"

The doctor looked stern before he answered. "I'm afraid that she's been arrested for murder and is in police custody."

"Oh, dear God. She didn't do it, but I know who did," he moaned.

"That's a matter for the law. Our job is to make sure you recover from this injury."

"I need to talk to the police right away. Get them here because it's imperative!"

"They came to speak to you earlier, but you were sleeping. I told them to come back again to see you."

"This is a matter of life and death! Literally! Get them here! Now!" exclaimed Carlton and then winced with pain.

"All right, all right, Mr Flint. I'll do my best for you, but calm down," appeased the doctor.

Carlton sucked in the air as a fresh wave of pain shot through his back. Randal felt the searing hot needles by proxy and groaned along with Carlton. It almost took his breath away.

I'll just lie low in his head and see what he tells the police. This should be really entertaining. I may as well enjoy the second half of the show. From my VIP private brainbox.

As the consultant left Carlton's room, Detective Inspector Wayne Bredbury, accompanied by his sergeant, were already heading towards him.

"Are you looking after Carlton Flint?" asked the detective.

"Yes. He's literally just asked me to contact you. Apparently, he urgently needs to talk."

"Is he up to it?"

"He's very agitated, so try not to overtire him. He's had a serious injury, although he's recovering well."

Both policemen nodded and entered the room.

Carlton was breathing heavily, partly due to the pain but mostly over Francine's arrest. A nurse was administering an injection, so they waited until she had finished. Carlton waved them over and before they actually reached his bedside, he launched into verbal action.

"How's my wife, Officer? I'm out of my mind with worry

about her. She's totally innocent. You have to believe me!" he almost begged.

"Regrettably your wife is very disturbed, Mr Flint. She's openly admitted to murdering Dr Winston Ramsey and Stella Reid. She has also confessed her intentions to kill you. She was extremely clear about it all."

Carlton licked his dry lips and his voice cracked as he spoke. "*He* made her say those words. *He* engineered the whole horrific, gruesome, tragedy. She was hypnotised and used in a telepathic, murderous atrocity," he gasped.

"He? Who is he? Who made her say those words, Mr Flint? Who made her do it, as you emphatically state?"

"The psychotic, satanic, accursed demon who masquerades under the name of Randal Forbes! That's who!"

"Randal Forbes? You mean the famous author and entrepreneur? Why should he wish to harm your family and friends, or yourself for that matter? Are you saying he was another guest? As far as we know from your daughter, there was nobody else invited to your house that evening."

"He wasn't there in the flesh. But he was inside my wife's head."

Inspector Bredbury looked at his sergeant. He thought that Carlton was as deranged as Francine, but he still let him speak.

"You simply have to understand. Randal Forbes is a psychotic psychic. He has the absolute power to enter a victim's head and control their minds, force them to do monstrous things to themselves, or to each other. His speciality is cold-blooded, telepathic murder."

"With respect, Mr Flint, we know that you're a famous astrologer. Are you sure you're not getting carried away with your theories?"

"Oh, God. This isn't an astrological matter. I've never revealed this before, but I need to save my wife from the greatest injustice that could ever befall her. I also have a gift outside of astrology. I'm telepathic and can affect circumstances and people with my own mind. I've kept this side of me totally hidden from everyone. The difference between Randal Forbes and myself is that I use the same powers to help the human race. He uses his powers to kill them!"

The two officers looked at each other again and Randal saw the absolute disbelief on their faces through Carlton's eyes.

They think you're as cuckoo as your moonstruck wife. You're digging a black hole for yourself, except I'm the one who'll bury you in it. Carry on, starman. They'll end up sectioning you as well.

"Mr Flint. I hope you realise how far-fetched your theory sounds. I repeat, your wife has made a full statement that she intended to kill you, as well as the two deceased people."

"And I need you to realise how much evidence I can give you against Randal Forbes! Your fellow consultant physician, my dear friend Dr Winston Ramsey, was well aware of the truth. He helped me heal myself both psychically and physically while I was comatose. He knew the full extent of Randal's crimes and wanted to see him brought to justice. *That's* why Randal killed him."

"Your wife killed him, Mr Flint, with a meat cleaver. The same axe that nearly killed yourself, but the blow wasn't strong enough to finish the job and you survived."

"*No!* Randal Forbes killed them, possibly with his daughter's help!"

"His daughter?"

"Yes! His daughter! Roxanne! She's his doppelganger. Together they are team lethal. She's almost eight years old but very powerful. He's coached her well."

Inspector Bredbury shook his head. "Mr Flint, you must know how all this sounds. It's as far removed from the reality of the situation that it could possibly be. Surely you don't expect the law to accuse someone of multiple murders on this whimsical evidence? I was in the room when your wife confessed. It's as straight-forward as that."

"Just exactly what did she say to you?" asked Carlton in a very strained voice.

"That you and Stella Reid were having an affair and were planning to kill her for the life insurance money. Also, Dr Ramsey was an accomplice. She was uncontrollable one minute and completely tranquil the next as she confessed. She added that the Scarlet Pimpernel helped her and told her to put caustic soda into your drinks to weaken you. Quite frankly, she's one very disturbed lady."

Carlton swallowed hard. He was full of hatred and loathing for Randal and deep concern for Francine. "Don't you see? Randal Forbes is the Scarlet Pimpernel! It's an alias he used, a hypnosis he engineered, so that my wife would not recognise him and be completely under his control. He's had it in for me from the second we were introduced through his cousin Dean Gibson, who is controller of programmes at Astral TV. Randal owns the company. He cannot stand the fact that I have the same level of power as him – more so, that I use mine for good. The upshot is that he and his daughter Roxanne want me dead. They tried once before and failed by causing that monster monitor to fall on my head in the last *Celestial Bodies* programme."

"I remember that show; it went out live. Was Randal Forbes present?"

"He was, but behind the scenes he was plotting my demise with his daughter. They are livid that I'm still breathing. So, he concocted another homicidal drama by using and manipulating my wife, the last person on earth who I would suspect."

"If all of this is remotely true, then why hasn't anyone else come forward before to implicate him in a crime?"

"Simple. He got to them all and removed them. There's a list of victims as long as the Amazon. He's been performing his deadly rituals since he was a child. He's abominable. Completely and undoubtedly insane," gasped Carlton.

Both policemen looked disbelievingly at Carlton as his doctor came into the room with a nurse.

"I think Mr Flint should rest now. He's still weak and needs as much breathing space as he can get. I have to call a halt to the conversation on both sides."

"OK, but we'll come back again when he's more rested. We do need to question him further, but we'll leave it alone for now," agreed the detective, as Randal smirked.

Oh, I'm enjoying this so much. In fact, I'm having such fun that I'm going to share this pivotal moment with him. So here we go.

Ground control to Starman Flint. Your words are falling on deaf, disbelieving ears. Do you really think they're going to swallow your dark fairy stories? You've got as much chance of convincing them as Rip Van Winkle suffering from insomnia.

Carlton's head jerked from side to side. His facial expression changed into an ugly snarl as he accommodated Randal's sardonic possession.

"Don't go! Don't leave the room! All of you, come back! He's in my head right now and he's heard every single word we've said. His cruel, acidic, sarcastic, repulsive wit has come out to play!"

"He's in your head?"

He knows that you don't believe me and it's an enormous high for him. He wants you to think I'm unhinged, and if you walk away from me disbelievingly, that will be the biggest kick of all for him."

"Mr Flint, you can't possibly expect me to believe all this."

"I'm telling you! He's still plotting to kill me! Even if my wife is found guilty of the whole atrocity, he will still come after me. Then you'll know she's innocent of all this madness. But I don't want that to happen! I want her with me! She's the victim, not the perpetrator!"

Inspector Bredbury thought that Carlton and Francine Flint were on mind-altering drugs. Randal smirked uncontrollably behind Carlton's eyes as both policemen left the room, shaking their disbelieving heads.

Oh, this is getting better by the second. Keep waffling, wittering and wailing, and they'll lock you both up in neighbouring padded cells. You could send love notes to each other through the bars.

You could do the horoscopes of the other inmates. Tell them who'll get on with who and why. Earth signs with neon signs and all that rot. You could even predict when they'll be let out.

What size straight-jacket do you take, Carlton? You're going to need one.

Randal felt as if he was covered in mystical itching powder causing a tingling sensation on the surface of his skin. Every pore responded to his psychic arousal because he knew that Carlton's life on earth was nearing its end, and this time there would be no shortfall or incomplete operation.

Through Carlton's eyes, Randal had acquired a photographic image of his nurse which he fed into his own cranial computer. Randal's head was jam-packed with data which remained inside his human inbox, filed away into past, present and future folders.

Roxanne was also in a state of high expectancy. She knew that her father was warming up to bring the Flint saga to its inevitable conclusion. She thoroughly approved of his plan to rid them both of their most formidable enemy to date. She had tried twice to end his reign and failed, but she had weakened him and now he was vulnerable.

Once again Randal's barbaric sense of acrimony came out to gambol. He could not resist a final telepathic taunt. So, he slipped into Carlton's head again effortlessly.

Wakey, wakey, Starman! I just thought I'd fill you in on the latest news! Your wacko wife's just flown over the cuckoo's nest and is still non compos mentis. I think a plea of diminished responsibility will be her best chance of being released next century. Give or take a day or two, maybe. Take your pick.

Carlton's head felt trashed. The pain in his back was still

severe. Randal had cruelly caused it to escalate by pressing his long, slim fingers into the rear of Carlton's full-length photograph, like a kind of damaging acupressure.

Carlton replied telepathically, but he was debilitated.

Oh, you mad, detestable, crazy piece of crap. My wife's in hell, your home ground! As soon as I get out of here, you're dead.

Brave words, starman. What makes you think you're going to get out? It's curtains, and I don't mean the ones around your hospital bed.

You keep telling yourself that and you'll believe it. It's not going to happen. I'm here to stay and I'll disclose your polluted insanity to the world. You're dead. Oh so dead and on display!

Am I now?

One hundred per cent deceased. So, watch your back.

Talking about backs, how's your pain today? Is it a little more, shall we say, rigorous?

Randal compressed his fingers into the flipside of Carlton's photographic image, causing him to cry out in pain.

Is that a cry of agony or ecstasy? Pray tell.

Get a life, Randal. A million miles away from mine.

Oh, I intend to.

Now leave me alone.

My pleasure.

Randal gave Carlton the impression of vacating his mind, but he was still occupying a small space in his subconscious. He exacerbated his suffering by the constant telepathic poking and prodding of his fingers, until Carlton pressed the buzzer for help.

The nurse sprang to attention and saw that he needed another pain-killing injection.

She filled the syringe with morphine, but just before she administered the treatment, Randal spoke to her mind. She held the hollow tube in the air and looked at the amount. Then she upped the dose at Randal's command.

Carlton was writhing in agony, begging her to help him.

She stuck the sharp needle into his arm and plunged the liquid medication into his bloodstream.

At first it was the most remedial, efficacious surge of relief, but then his heartbeat became rapid. Its pace was ridiculously off the scale until he thought it would burst through his chest. He struggled to breathe and clutched his breast as his body began the process of shutting down.

His life flashed before him. Forty years of living, in a minute's wrestle to survive. The nurse just stood by and watched. She was under strict instructions to do nothing. She just checked her nails and noticed that the one on her index finger was chipped.

She tutted to herself. "That's what you get with cheap nail varnish. It ruins them." She spoke out loud.

Randal stayed inside her head until Carlton's very last heartbeat flatlined. He caused all machinery to stall. The nurse stood on the spot, staring into space.

Randal pulled out of both their heads when he saw that Carlton had gone for good.

You know what, I'm actually going to miss you, starman, in the most perverse way. But you see, it was only ever going to end like this.

Reconciliation was just not feasible. But let me give you some credit. You put up one hell of a galactic battle. Full marks for that.

Now I'm going to tell my inheritress that you've finally flown to the big asteroid in the sky. That you'll be blinking down on us from one of your planets. I never did find out your sun sign. Shucks.

So long then, old foe. 'The gift' has finally triumphed and now belongs solely to the designated receivers once more. You truly were the imposter. But now you've made way for the correct beneficiaries: myself and Roxanne.

The only true recipients of our glorious benefaction.

EPILOGUE

Tyrone Pendle was alone in his bedroom, reading a newspaper as he sipped his cream soda.

Carlton Flint's death was dominating the headlines, along with his incarcerated wife. Tyrone frowned and wrinkled his cute nose for added effect. He smelt a big, fat rat.

When he had watched Carlton on *Celestial Bodies*, he could never stand the holy expression on his face. He had felt like punching it in.

Righteousness on two loathsome legs.

But he knew instinctively that Carlton had possessed real powers and had the gift of telepathic transmission. That is why he had watched the programme each week, but Carlton's benevolence had always stuck in Tyrone's throat. The stench of devoutness permeated his airways.

When the heavy screen had crashed down on the back of Carlton's head, live on television, Tyrone had just laughed. Inwardly, of course. Not openly to his family, who were sat with him on the expensive settee. They had screamed with shock at the gruesome spectacle before them.

Tyrone's large brown eyes began to glow. For thirteen years he had lived with this secret, not knowing if there was anyone else out there with the same curse: a mind-blowing curse that had held him back because he was too shaken to reveal it. Not to his parents, or to his siblings.

And yet underneath all the fear and trepidation, he had always felt vastly superior to the masses, but as he had nobody to discuss his sixth sense with, he had hidden it behind a façade of reasonable normality.

Until now. Until he saw his saviour being interviewed as part of a Carlton Flint tribute programme. Until his own startling gaze became fixed upon his would-be helper's other-worldly, striking face.

Tyrone knew that here lay the answer to his discarded prayers. A six-foot two-inch vision of darkness, with a smile that lit up the dispirited room, with eyes that flared into his own and spoke to him of dangerous, decadent and magical things.

Here was his deepest, fathomless, immaterial awakening. A kindred dark spirit who could show him the way to ethereal salvation. A councillor who would commiserate with his years of stunted, paranormal progress.

Just look at him. He's amazing! All my so-called friends are into stupid, brainless hobbies. They're so thick. But I'm like him. Special. I need to see him. I can feel his powers through the screen. I'm only young. Maybe I have to be older when I meet him.

I know. I'll wait a few more years. Yeah. That's it. Then I can talk on his level. He won't take notice of a kid. But when I'm a man, then he'll know I'm like him. He's either gonna like me or see me as a threat. But I want to be his equal. I want him to show me the right way to use my magic. I can wait.

Tyrone had always longed to use his powers without introspection. He needed a guide to light up his wickedness. Permission to reveal his baseness. He craved the freedom to be his absolute true sinful self.

He longed for the encouragement to turn his curse into a gift. To know that he was not alone in his woeful desires.

And now his wish had come true and he needed to be near him. To be with him.

As his teacher. His mentor. His master.

Randal Forbes!

About the Author

Fran Raya currently lives in Manchester. Her career has been predominantly in music since the 1970s, both in the UK and abroad, originally as a singer-songwriter but now in later years purely as a songwriter who places original songs with other artists. Fran is a member of The Guild of International Songwriters and Composers (GISC) and has been featured in their quarterly magazines. She has performed throughout Europe as she used to be based in Denmark and was the support act for Eric Clapton on his Scandinavian tours in the 1980s. She has also published poetry in numerous anthologies and as a result was awarded her own book, Thoughts of the Poet.

For writing and publishing news, or recommendations of new titles to read, sign up to the Book Guild newsletter: